A Dragon's Miracle: Gay Dragon MPREG Romance

Van Cole

Published by Van Cole, 2022.

A DRAGON'S MIRACLE: GAY DRAGON MPREG ROMANCE

First edition. November 29, 2022.

Copyright © 2022 Van Cole.

ISBN: 979-8223027409

Written by Van Cole.

Table of Contents

A Dragon's Miracle
Gay Dragon MPREG Romance

By: Van Cole

By: Van Cole

Foreword

Being a dragon is hard enough, but being a gay one is even harder.

River is a young man getting to grips with the double whammy of being a dragon shifter as well as gay, in the small backwater of Carlsbad.

To make matters worse, he accidentally comes out as both gay and a dragon, at his graduation party, without realizing it.

Now shunned by the townsfolk, his father decides to send him away, under the tutelage of the charismatic, but also very strange, Storm Woods.

Despite an initial attraction to each other, he and River have many adversaries to overcome before the path to happiness is open to either of them.

But will shadows of the past put their emergent relationship in danger? And do they even have a relationship in the first place?

And when a shocking revelation is made, how will either River or Storm cope with its implications?

A Dragon's Miracle

Chapter 1

River

Carlsbad doesn't feel like home, anymore.

Thinking back about it, I'm not sure it ever did.

It's such a clichéd way to think, but I cannot conjure anything more creative while I drive to Ricker's, the only little grocery store left in a place best described as a functioning ghost town. A zombie town, rather, if you want to emphasize the living in its deadness.

Ricker's is a zombie hut like every other place, animated but unmistakably deceased.

There used to be more like it - Burt's on East and Lucky's on South, but eight years of the unrecovered recession put boards on Burt's windows and red, chipping CLOSED signs in Lucky's entryways. Big-name retailers and dad's go-to, Ricker's on Main, are among the only stores – the only places, in fact – left operating.

Many times, I have wished that my dad would clear out of here and move somewhere else. Anywhere else.

I'm not sure what binds him to this place like glue.

It's not like it's family, that's for certain.

Because it's only the two of us, at the moment. That is me and my dad.

Memory guides my steering, and I study the line of houses to my right. Once palatial mansions, they, like the businesses that surround them, have withered as money – or what Carlsbad considers money – sought bigger, more tenable opportunities in the cities that ate up Carlsbad's already unsteady economy. Starting in my teenage years, companies came to accept that no one younger than retirement age wanted to stay in a place that offered young job-seekers, at best, minimum wage.

Many of my classmates have moved away. In a way, so have I. To college, but like a bad penny, I keep turning up here, on the streets of Carlsbad.

I must go somewhere in the vacation and anyway, my father is expecting me to take over the helm at his fireplace business in a few years' time.

Anyway, the place is even more desolate than I remember when I left for the start of the semester and that was only a few months ago.

Another boarded up building, which was once an impressive detached family home. The white picket fence at the front has already fallen into disrepair. The grass lawn, which had previously been pruned to within an inch of its life by its' proud owner now grew wild and straggly.

In fact, the owner hadn't seen the light and headed for the bright lights and wanton attractions of Springfield up the road, he had succumbed to the hole in the ground. Or in the sky, depending on your beliefs, either way, he had preferred to stay here and die than move away to anywhere more promising.

God. Twenty years old, and I already sound like my father.

He, Ashton Marsh, heritor and current owner of Marsh Home & Hearth, stayed in Carlsbad thanks to his father and grandfather's genius.

Somehow, in the days of yore, the two foresaw our ancient collective, also known as Carlsbad County, keeping its fireplaces. And, as the old saying goes, if there's a fireplace, someone will need to service it.

I guess my dad is just as bad as those that he criticizes. After all, he sticks around and I suppose, in a sort of way, so have I.

So, the Marsh men stuck around and came as close to being a celebrity as possible in a place where a fun night out consists of drive-through burgers, driving circles around the park and, after age eighteen, insurmountable quantities of alcohol.

And I don't say "Marsh men" because of an old-fashioned, no-women-allowed-in-business sentiment, either. It's serious because no one in my family, as far as I can remember, has been a woman.

Only male children have been born for generations now.

Added to that, women don't seem to have been too lucky in our family, either.

My father raised me alone after my mom died in childbirth.

My great-grandfather raised my grandfather on his own, in a time when understanding anything about children was taboo.

My grandfather raised my dad on his own, in similar circumstances, with the Cold War as a bonus. This was after my grandmother died when my dad was still young, but at least he had known her. Slightly.

You would have thought all this practice would have made the males in our family up to speed when it came to child rearing, especially the preparing their sons for the future.

But unfortunately, that isn't really the case at all.

As you will probably find out if you carry on reading this.

Luckily, even in Carlsbad, things had turned around once I was born. Regardless of whether this change came from urban sprawl or a truly miraculous paradigm change on the town's part, my father had the joy of raising a son who was – and still is – a dragon and gay, in relative privacy.

Did I not mention I am a dragon?

The Marsh family descends from a long line of dragon shifters. Yeah, that adds a twist to the small-town family tale, but our origins date back to antiquity. The whole antiquity thing is where stuff gets muddled because, of course, no one kept comprehensive records a thousand years ago. Still, my father swears up and down that our branch started in Ireland. Perhaps the countless fairy tales and dragon-based role-play games gave him a clue.

I know that his mother, my grandmother came from Ireland. But since my dad rarely if ever talks about her – or any of our family for that matter, I don't know much about her or them.

Thankfully, I don't need to spend much time in the past to talk about being a shifter in the present; in the Marsh house, we've never been big on tradition or rituals.

This could be an understatement.

For instance, I live a normal life, for the most part: as normal as it gets somewhere like Carlsbad.

I'm going to school for management in a town about an hour away, which is no bigger than Carlsbad, but way livelier. I get good grades there, too, except in Spanish (I suck at Spanish).

Furthermore, according to my college buddies, I'm an expert at entertaining crushes on people who will have nothing to do with me.

Maybe I'm not serious about them ever transpiring into anything. I don't know. There have never been any romantic liaisons on the horizon whilst I've been there, but at least it has taken me out of the claustrophobic confines of Carlsbad.

As far as my management studies are going, it is all good. I suppose my final destination is a done deal, I will be returning to the fold when it's all over.

So, yeah. My life is relatively normal all in all, or at least I've been trying hard to make it so, given all the... irregularities... there are.

Plus, even though my dad owns a business, I've taken a few jobs outside the family trade because I want to vary my résumé.

I would be lying to say that varying my résumé wasn't dad's idea. I declared my major two years ago, and always intended to return to Carlsbad after college. Despite the town's downfalls, I feel obliged to stay because no one, at least in my circle of knowledge, wants to manage fireplace repair services. I imagine it's too niche.

Chapter 2

River

I approach Ricker's. A fresh gust of wind blows some golden-brown leaves into the windscreen and a few come in through the open window.

As I pull up the beauty of the season washes over me, momentarily.

Sometimes it's easy to forget the everyday picturesque nature of our, very ordinary, boring little town.

Tonight, a gorgeous display of pinks and grays intermingle in the evening sky.

The color resonates over the whole town and everything basks in its aura. The unlovely shop front of Ricker's even looks momentarily cozy.

It's large, red sign glows in the late fall sunset, and its fluorescent lights glow beyond its window-paneled face. I park the car and lock its door, lowering my head as I enter the store to avoid detection. This will be a quick in-and-out. All we need is milk.

Yet the cashier, possibly an old classmate, recognizes me. Her eyes glow fiercely across the store as if to say, 'welcome back, freak'.

I look at my toes and shove my hands in my pockets, wishing the milk would materialize before me so I can pay and leave.

Sometimes, I wonder why I think Carlsbad no longer feels like home when it holds my family and my only hope of a successful future.

Each time, I think it will be different when I come back here. That one day they will forget like my dad said they would.

But then, every time I return from school, I feel the stares and hear the whispers.

It is all still there as if it is never going away.

And what is my dreadful crime amongst my ex-classmates and one-time friends?

Well, you might be guessing that in a place like Carlsbad no one ever forgets a damn thing and that any tiny little incidences take on biblical significance.

This would be true. This petty little town is built on feuds and spats, grown up over generations. Local reputations have been forged and cast in iron over some incidental remark, said in jest, over twenty years ago.

If it is one thing the citizens of Carlsbad have really made their own, it is the completely out of proportion beef.

However, in my case, the reason for my classmates' coolness has some more basis in fact. I mean, from their point of view, it was a pretty big deal.

And mine, too.

All this bad feeling resonates from two years ago when I mistakenly revealed that I was a dragon at my own graduation party.

Chapter 3

Ashton

He may be a man, but he's still my boy.

River leaves to get the milk. The cabin makes for close quarters and, no matter how thick our insulation, words just seem to travel. Finally, during his brief outing, I can pick up the phone without hesitation and make the call that I knew, deep down, I would someday have to make.

Feeling hesitant, I wonder if it will even be answered. If he is even still at the same place.

Am I even doing the right thing calling him at all?

Storm, to my surprise, answers despite my long-distance number. Perhaps he's used to answering to the unknown, after all, his clientele varies with the season. Perhaps I caught him in the down season. As I haven't seen or spoken with him in ages, I cannot imagine what patterns his work must follow.

I ask him if he remembers me, a dumb question given our history. A small growl, which I detect over the receptor, tells me he recognizes my voice before I say my name.

I should have known that he would do. I have been in touch, fleetingly, over the years, but it has always been to talk shop. This time, I need to discuss a personal matter.

And this is something that makes me nervous. ...Discussing anything of that nature with Storm. I can only hope that over the intervening years he has mellowed somewhat and is less likely to resent my intrusion.

He is the only person I can really think of to help with this matter and I have been wracking my brains about it for a long time.

Oddly enough, he asks first about my father. I tell him that yes; Silus Marsh went away in his sleep, as crotchety as he had been in his old age.

Storm sighs over the receiver.

"Thank God. I can finally live without that weight on my shoulders."

I ask him what he means, only for him to clam up.

My own dragon senses haven't withered, however; one of the most important men in home design still feels the merciless burn of my own father's homophobia, something that even I have forgiven.

What happened back then happened. It's all water under the bridge now. Maybe things might have been uncomfortable between us for a while, but surely, now we are both proper grown-ups, at the helm of our own empires, surely, we should be able to put the past behind us?

However, hearing Storm's emotion seeping out, regarding my father brings it all flooding back.

How long has it been? Over twenty years at least, but it still feels awkward discussing our private business. I suppose I'm still not used to it at the best of times.

Since River's mother died I haven't really had much practice at conducting any kind of personal business. Hearing Storm caught so unawares like this has put me on the back foot.

I begin to confront the man's insecurities but, I console myself, this call isn't about that.

But because I don't know how long River will be, I must move the conversation along.

So quickly, without any preamble I tell Storm first that I have a son, adding perspective to the depth of our conversations over the past two decades.

There is a slight silence.

I wonder how he is digesting this fact.

"Well, belated congratulations," he says coolly. "So, how old is he?"

The man's question bounces forth from the other end of the line.

"He's twenty. He's in his sophomore year of college."

Now I can hear him doing the mental arithmetic. Yes, it was obviously after we.... Whatever happened. When I moved on and eventually married River's mom.

"Did he, um," Storm searches for words. He must have his posse near. "Did he inherit anything?"

"Yes," I can't help but smile at the awkwardness of the conversation. Phones and the fear of being overheard had added a whole new layer to the double-entendres.

"Yes," I continue, "and that's what I'm calling about."

"Don't tell me," Storm interrupts, "he doesn't want to sweep chimneys for a living."

I cannot tell if the man jokes or is serious.

Since his rise to fame, Storm has – understandably so – grown less fond of our kind; less considerate of businessmen such as myself. Living in another world, however, makes such changes expected.

I assume my friend has employed his typical sarcasm.

"No," I snap with a laugh and mock an English accent. "He's a dedicated chimney sweeper, the best in all of London."

I then turn serious;

"Every time he comes back from school, he seems sadder, less outgoing, and less confident."

"Maybe," Storm says flippantly, "you're over thinking it. Depression in college isn't weird, Ashton, it's like one in five people or something. Not that you would know, but maintaining grades and a social life isn't exactly easy."

After all this time, Storm still hasn't managed to let me forget that he was the one that went on to study at a fancy college and I wasn't. That he was the one who left for pastures new and I was the deadbeat that stayed.

This was part of the reason I was so keen for River to go away to school. To broaden his horizons, spread his wings, do more than I had done.

The thing was, he had gotten all these opportunities but still hadn't seemed to completely embrace them. On the surface of it, things were going well. Except to see him, it didn't seem that way.

And possibly because nowadays I was seeing him less often, I was getting to see the changes in him more notably.

I tried not to let Storm's dismissal of the problem show in my voice, but it was not easy.

Reminding myself that Storm could hardly be blamed for not realizing the crux of the matter immediately about a boy he had never met, I plowed ahead.

"I get that. He sounds fine at school, though. He has a lot of friends there."

"Then, what's the problem?" he asked.

There was an insouciance in his voice that irritated me. I had been hoping for Storm's full attention. His serious appraisal of the situation. Not what seemed to amount to a blanket dismissal.

Never mind, I continued anyway.

"Well, he," I lower my voice, fearing my son's return, "he had a mishap a few years ago, at his graduation party."

The interior designer sighs;

"Aren't all small-town graduation parties their own sort of mishap?"

It's like I see him roll those all too cool eyes on the end of the phone line. In fact, I can just picture his smug, urbane face, especially whilst talking to someone like me whom he considers practically a hillbilly these days.

Who needs Skype? I already want to wipe that self-assured look off his face now.

"I don't mean like that,"

Now my irritation begins to show; despite trying I can't stop it from leaking out into our conversation.

How can I convey this to him quickly and succinctly? Before either River returns and catches the end of this call or someone on the other end overhears him.

Momentarily, I think that it would serve him right if they did do.

Cultured, superior Storm still needing to hide the truth from those around him. Even there, as the supposed big cheese in his own cheese counter, he had to be careful who was listening.

And for all his sneering about me and then my father's small-town homophobia. There are still things he cannot discuss in public.

"I mean, he did it, if you catch my drift. He," I turn my voice to a whisper, "shifted."

"He–, he what?"

"It's not like he didn't inherit something. He gets genes from both sides, Storm. I knew from day one this would happen, and," I put my hand over my face, "it's partly my fault. I never taught him to shift properly."

It was true. With my own son, I had neglected one of the most critical duties of dragon parents: the shift.

Carlsbad's conservative nature had wormed its way into my very core and implanted, without my awareness, the sinister idea that my son would somehow forget his shifter identity if he ignored it long enough...

I suppose this is pretty much what my own father did with me. You might say that our family was not big on traditions. But, I guess we did have one of our own. That of sweeping things under the carpet and hoping for the best.

I had figured out the basics of shifting on my own, without any parental guidance. Therefore, I had simply assumed that River would work it out on his own.

It is not like I am some expert shifter or golden dragon, but I can get by. The truth is, I am pretty isolated from any dragon community around here. That's if there even exists one here anymore. I suppose I wouldn't really know.

Which is what has led me to being forced into making this call, right now, to the only person who I can think of who might be able to help.

How has it come to this, I think, that the sole person to whom I can turn to for advice after all this time is Storm?

That, in the intervening twenty years, I have not forged one close relationship with another man – dragon or no – to speak to about anything.

I guess I have thrown myself into my work and tried to throw myself into the respectable façade of the community.

Don't laugh.

Carlsbad has a sort of respectable business community and I have successfully inveigled myself into it.

Unfortunately, being respectable doesn't mean I have anyone to speak to about close personal matters. In fact, when they are ones like this, it especially means that I don't have anyone to speak to about them.

Right now, I am hearing a voice hiss in my ear, berating me for not keeping in closer touch with Storm or – hell – with anyone from the dragon shifting community.

It shouldn't really have been rocket science, to have pre-empted any of the bumps in the road that I was bound to come across with a teenage son.

I should have thought better, and I should have parented smarter. The animals in the fields have shown us that nothing comes of stifling instinct.

I explained these faults to Storm, who made no sound on the other end of the receiver.

My only excuse was that I had no better example to follow than the one that my own father had given me.

Well, at that I could once again practically see Storm's left eyebrow raise in smug righteousness. He would have loved that one.

Yes, if it is one tradition that the Marsh family seem proud to keep upholding it is that of consistent half-assed parenting.

I tried to get through my tale of woe as quickly as possible, given the fact River could be back here any minute.

At the end of what I could only call a flood of self-pity, he flatly questioned:

"Why are you calling me about it?"

Well, I knew that one was coming.

Why was I calling him after such a long time? That is what he really meant.

More to the point, how dare I call him about something like this without even telling him that I had a son in the first place.

Or tell him anything personal after I suspended all contact. I guess he hadn't quite still forgiven me. ...Forgiven my father for that one.

The fact the first question he had chosen to ask me was about Silus, said it all. I noted that he hadn't asked me about River's mom. I guess that was too much of a sticking point for him still.

Who would have thought it after all this time, that traces of bitterness would still show with him?

And who would have thought that after all this time, it was still to Storm that I turned with any sort of problem?

"You're my closest contact, and you and River have a lot in common."

I didn't want to tell him that I had cut myself off from the other shifters over the past two decades, which I sought to protect my career and my reputation in this small, incredibly nosy town. I didn't want to tell him that leaving was, as he had told me those years before, the best decision anyone from Carlsbad could make.

Storm made his own skepticism clear.

"Yeah, we're special," he went on, an eye-roll drifting off his tongue. "So, what? Aren't there other special people you could pass him along to? He has to have other relatives."

Well, not really. But since he hadn't asked about his mother, he wouldn't know.

He did know that I came from a long, but not incredibly fecund, line of shifters. Meaning, I had no siblings, uncles or even cousins with whom to beg a favor off.

But was there more to this line of questioning than just enquiring about our lineage?

Was he really asking me whether I regretted breaking things off – such as they were – between us?

Because if it was, then the answer was still going to be no.

And I wasn't sure if an ego like Storm was up for hearing that, just yet.

Even though I didn't regret anything that had happened or more to the point, hadn't happened – it didn't change the fact that after twenty years and only a handful of phone calls about the pitfalls of fireplaces in modern interior design – that he was still my closest acquaintance.

More than this though, the penny obviously had not dropped that there was more to the meaning of my phone call than talking him through River's shifter status.

I decided to give him every detail.

"River," I said, "is more than just a shifter,"

I accented the word as evidence I was alone.

"River's also gay. I would like for you to take him under your wing for a while. Show him that there's more than Carlsbad after college."

"In college," Storm sounded uneasy, "what does he do?"

"He's in management," I replied, "and you can keep him if he does well."

This had been something that I had had to think long and hard about.

I mean, I knew that River would jump at the chance of getting out of here if he had the opportunity. What kid wouldn't?

And that was one who didn't have the unfortunate reputation of turning into a fire-breathing dragon at his own graduation.

What I had to think long and hard about was my own selfish desires to keep him around me. But gradually, seeing him coming home, more and more despondent had made me realize it was inevitable.

As for trusting Storm to ensure his side of the bargain was kept honorably? Well. I guess there must have been still a part of me that had enough faith in him.

He would be able to show River the ropes, as it were. He would be able to introduce him to the right people and the right places in a big city.

He would guide his way and help him find a suitable partner somewhere and relax into adult life.

He would also hopefully be able to help him become comfortable with his identity as both a dragon and a gay man.

Because I knew I was asking a hell of a lot, I had to sweeten the deal by offering him something to make it worth his while.

And River had the ability to be a good manager. His grades were good in college and he had quite a talent for the business.

He could really shape up to be an asset for Storm's business.

"Hmmm"

There was a pause on the line. Storm was tempted, I could tell it.

The proposition pushed Storm into something that sounded like an agreement, and just in time: I heard the gravel crumbling under the slow-rolling wheels of River's car.

Chapter 4

River

In Carlsbad and towns like it, graduating high school calls for nothing less than bacchanalia. I admit I fell victim to this mindset.

Excited about throwing the society party of the season, I had spent hours arranging the patio, making sure it looked like something between an old English séance and a cover from a copy of Better Homes and Gardens that my father never read, but refused to throw away. Having arranged two dozen plastic lawn chairs around a large, wrought-iron fire pit, I hung garlands of fairy lights and silky streamers of fabric to garnish the scene.

I had never had a party before and was amazed that my father had granted permission for one.

In my circle of friends, house parties still didn't happen that regularly and so the anticipation of the event chez Marsh was the news in Carlsbad for what felt like months.

Naturally, more people had ended up on the invite list than I had originally intended and more guests turned up than had been invited.

My guess is that at one point there must have been a couple of hundred kids there, many of them I didn't recognize.

I had made my dad clear out for the duration of the party as he would have been freaked to see the numbers rising and rising.

In all honesty, it could have been worse and the place didn't get completely trashed. But it would be untrue to say there wasn't a bit of scarring to the property.

Most of the worst scars ended up being my own, mental ones though.

Back to the day of the party though. I was on a roll. Full of excitement and teenage angst about how it would turn out.

Whether that cute guy that I had my eye on would show up and whether he would be suitably impressed with me and my hospitality to allow me to get a bit closer, than the vague smiles we were giving to each other around the place.

So, I had decked the garden out in all the fairy lights from Christmas and tried to set the scene as best as I could.

But my plans didn't stop there. Since this was a private, unsupervised party, the fire pit in question was placed a safe distance from a full, open bar whose provisions would give me the courage to maybe, even flirt with someone.

In the coolness of the dark summer night, it seemed like my party was a hit. Huddled around the fire pit, toasting marshmallows and drinking, I managed to catch the eye of more than one handsome stranger.

This, for Carlsbad, was quite a success. Of course, I was not really 'out' in public and so except for a very select few, no one knew that I was gay. At least, at the start of the party. And I was hoping to keep it that way too.

The drinks were flowing freely and I was just beginning to unwind enough to congratulate myself for daring to host this party.

Not being exactly the life and soul of the Carlsbad in crowd – or whatever constituted that – this had been the first thing that I had ever done in my life to make a statement socially.

And flirt, I did. Like I said, amazingly there were even more than one recipient of my heavy-handed ways.

But there was one boy who really attracted my attention.

The one from school. We had been giving each other these looks all over the place for weeks beforehand, but I had never spoken to him yet. He wasn't in any of my classes and I didn't even know his name at the time.

All I knew was that I liked the look of him and even more amazingly, he seemed to like the look of me or at least, managed not to be completely repelled by me.

His blond hair glowed like a halo around his delicately-featured face, and his infectious laugh chimed like bells in my hypersensitive ears. Yes, the alcohol might have accentuated his attractiveness, yet in the heat of the moment, he was no less than perfect.

Taking advantage of the fact that more alcohol was the inevitable solution to turning me from small town geeky nobody, into a special person of interest, I poured yet another beer down both of our necks, before beckoning him into somewhere a little quieter.

I had cultivated an environment that leaned itself to seduction. Music thrummed from amplified speakers, and the feverish, bouncing dance that ensued made catching a brush of the boy's smooth, ivory skin anything but difficult.

Soon, this mysterious stranger who, I admit, had intrigued me for weeks, had his hands about my waist. He whispered something about "real adults" into my ear, and nibbled at my neck.

That was all it took for my body to respond. The drink turned up the feelings I was experiencing, the hormones, the heat, the sweating. Before long, things were happening in my body that I didn't really understand and were completely beyond my control.

Between my own hot blush and the ravenous return of affection, I felt an unnatural heat begin to swell in my stomach. A rising, flickering sensation that I wasn't quite expecting...

However, I was also very drunk at that stage and didn't give it an awful lot of thought. I should have done though.

I stroked his hair and tried hard to focus properly. All I can remember was his vision of loveliness, a haze of blond and perfect, glistening skin. He felt soft and firm at the same time. And somehow, he had not run screaming from me just yet either.

We were fondling each other for I don't know exactly how long when once again, the burning heat inside my belly made itself known.

I might have even burped once or twice into the ear of my poor unwitting beloved.

I still wasn't too phased about it though.

Figuring the sensation came from the alcohol. I wouldn't really have known, never having reached this state of drunken dizziness before.

Sure, I had fallen into a merry daze in the past from one too many beers, but I had never hit the heights of drunken stupor like I did at this graduation party.

For a start off, there was the near-lethal punch bowl in the center of the room, which had just begged to be drunk from, as if it was some sort of ancient and sacred well.

I'm not sure how much had of it, but what does that matter when even one sip of it seemed to be enough to induce passing out and vomit on an epic scale.

All things considered, I thought I was doing pretty good to still be vertical. Not all my guests were holding up so well.

In fact, all over the house there were crashed out bodies, lying in a stupor and next to pools of their own bodily fluids.

Well, at that moment I was still congratulating myself for remaining conscious. The last things I remember before it all turned to shit was groggily leaning over my beau, intending to give him the kiss of his life.

I guess I probably did by all accounts. Just not the way either of us would ever have wanted it.

And man, the night had suddenly warmed up around me. It wasn't just the cloying closeness of alcohol-induced nausea I could feel. It was like real, actual, proper flames rising in my belly.

Assuming that this horrible heat was a result of alcohol, I did the only thing I could think of to help make it subside – by drinking yet more cool beer.

It didn't work. In fact. It just got worse.

The heat continued.

Then, I heard a yell.

Well, it was a scream. A proper blood-curdling scream.

Getting hotter and hotter inside of me, I didn't really know what was going on. I was uncomfortable, but somehow also unable to stop or deviate from my own erotic reverie.

More screaming.

The shrillness of that scream jolted me slightly out of my drunken high, but I soon returned to inebriated half-awareness.

I closed my eyes tighter. This I now believe constituted an effort to shut out whatever calamity passed around me.

In a drunken state like this, I wasn't even sure what was real and what was in my mind.

And I selfishly claimed the moment...

Only after I had done so did I notice that the object of my affections, the blond boy had gone.

Along with everyone else... He had run from sight and I was entirely alone.

It was only just beginning to dawn on me that something had gone very wrong.

Everything was blurred. My vision had altered, and I felt several feet higher in the air.

Like I was looking down on a scene of disaster from afar.

My heart began to race. I had ventured outside reality and found myself trapped. I could not return to the emergency.

I was simply stuck there, isolated in my strange state.

The screaming had now subsided and there was a deathly silence.

What had happened, where had they all gone? I still was not able to see properly - the world was very much out of focus.

And I had still not discovered my role in this collective distress. In fact, I was blissfully unaware that I had played any part in what had just happened.

It must all have been something else that someone else had done, I thought.

The strange sensation of being a few feet higher up and well, I don't know how to describe it, hadn't really set in yet. I was so inebriated, anything could be happening.

All I wanted to do was to come back down again. At that time, get back down meant come back to ground level and sober up. This must all be some alcoholic blackout, I thought.

I even thought that maybe someone had spiked the punch with LSD to make me feel like this.

Yeah, that must be it. This was all some sort of bad trip.

Wondering where everyone had gone, I groggily tried to get a grip of myself.

What the hell had just gone on here, to make everyone suddenly vamoose like that?

I still harbored the same high school fears, that someone had called the police or that someone, not knowing their limits, had gotten drunk enough to need medical attention.

There might be illegal drugs in the house – in my system. What if we got raided?

My dad would never live it down, being Mr. Respectable in this town.

My mind was still racing.

God, if only the emergency were so minor.

Fully opening my eyes, I found that I had not left reality.

I had left my clothes and my body though.

My clothes were lying at a sort of charred pile at the bottom of me.

Looking down, I was amazed to discover blue-and-green scales covered my arms, and my head stood several feet taller than my classmates'.

I had to blink a couple of times to make sure that this was real.

Well, okay, it seemed as if it was. My money was still on the LSD theory at that moment.

Oh, how I wished this could be so simply explained away by being spiked.

The thing was, now that I was starting to come around, I didn't really feel drugged anymore. My mind was beginning to clear and I was forced to acknowledge that the scene I was staring down at, might have some basis in reality.

A hot, ashy flavor crept into my throat, with a heat that I had mistaken for passion.

It was the same feeling that had occupied my stomach for all this time. I had tried to quench it with another drink. But it proved harder to put out a dragon's fire with tepid beer.

I, like most dragon shifters, later suffered from intense heartburn. But, in this instance, I could not mistake the taste of fire.

And I will never forget fire's taste, as well as the horror and embarrassment I sensed, of shifting before a crowd.

Because that is exactly what had happened and the horror of the situation was only just beginning to filter through to my brain.

The shock brought me quickly back to myself, but, drunk or not, I could not come down.

For what seemed like ages, I was just stuck there. Up in the air and unable to get back again.

And as for doing anything about it?

It was too late to make amends, and certainly too late to continue the party. The guests had fled in terror.

There was no way any of them would ever come back.

My father had told me I could shift from the time I was very young but had never told me how it happened. He failed to break that secrecy even as he helped me clean up the mess, assuring me only that, like everything in Carlsbad, the ordeal would blow over in a few months.

I guessed at some of the guilt he must have felt, at discovering me in that state.

He didn't even freak about the state of the house – and the few sleeping guests who lay in piles of their own vomit. The ones who had been so out of it that they had completely missed my little star turn.

Of course, they soon heard the full story. This was the stuff of legends, in a place like Carlsbad. Hell, this would have been enough to keep the rumor mill anywhere on earth rocking for all eternity.

Yeah. As if I didn't already know the seriousness of the situation, my father's quiet acceptance of it really cemented it.

He helped tidy up the mess without so much as one word of complaint or even, question, about anything that might have happened during the party.

It was so obviously bad there was no real point in picking over it more.

But if I was hoping for more information, the how, where and whys about shifting, then I was disappointed.

I mean, as it was, I was far too mortified to be asking any questions about what had just happened. I was spending most of my time in denial that it ever had and just hoping that the whole thing would go away.

But if my dad had brought the topic up, I would have been ready to listen.

However, he never did. I was still none the wiser as to what had happened or how.

He tried to cheer me along and promise me that there were more important things to think about than my unfortunate shift.

I had graduated high school and for all intents and purposes was getting out of here.

There was college to look forward to. Something that I had previously been half dreading as well as looking forward to.

I had been sad at the prospect of leaving all my friends and everyone that I knew in this two-bit town, but now, the chance of putting it all behind me couldn't come quick enough.

My father managed to persuade me that it didn't matter what anyone in this town might have thought. He said that they had short memories and anyway, no one would know who I was at college.

He was wrong on nearly every count.

I spent the rest of the summer getting ready for college, sticking by the assurance that everyone would forget what happened and that I could continue my "normal" life by winter break.

My father told me that the witnesses would soon be too preoccupied with their schoolwork to remember such an event and that they would see far stranger stuff coming from their fellow students. It was human nature, he told me, to forget. I believed him.

Obviously, that never happened.

Stranger than watching a drunken teenager turn into a scaly, fire-breathing dragon?

I doubt it comes stranger than that.

If I was lucky, the best I could hope for was others to have thought that they were witnessing some sort of collective delusion. Maybe they might think that they had been spiked by something in the punch after all.

Perhaps, a few of them did believe that. But the memory of that night was clearly something that was not going away, not ever.

I mean, this is the town where every little slight and perceived insult are remembered years later. As if something like this is ever going to be forgotten.

Now it is two years after my mistaken shift, and rumors have spread like wildfire.

I'm not only a dragon, I'm a monster with two counts – homosexuality and shifting – against me.

Mothers won't allow me near their children, and men of any age refuse to approach me.

To make this monster-horror tragedy even more clichéd, I no longer feel human.

Even in private, I still feel like the dragon freak.

And as for the escape to college? Well, I still went but it didn't stop the hurt or the intense loneliness I felt there.

Yes, I have some friends there, but it goes without saying that none of them know about the incident from two years previously.

But them not knowing doesn't make my room at college any more comforting, and it makes coming home, at best, a sobering experience.

Chapter 5

River

The memories of my failed party and its aftermath overwhelm me as I return with the milk.

I still don't like going out, for anything, when I return home. I certainly don't want to go anywhere where I might be recognized or that leads to human interaction.

It's him.

I can see the fear and the disgust in their eyes. Not even just the ones who were there at the party.

The rumors have spread through the whole town. To usually sober and careful people who wouldn't take the wild tales of drunken teens too seriously.

There were just too many kids telling the same story for it to be ignored. So now everyone and anyone, regardless of whether they had been there or not, met me with that look in their eyes.

Since going anywhere in this one-horse town seems to result in seeing someone and therefore, being shunned by them, it kind of puts you off leaving the house at all.

I slam my car door and walk up the back steps, onto the same patio where the accident happened.

Even beneath its new varnish and amid an icy cold of the fall turning into winter, the clay-tiled surface still recalls that fateful day. I paint the crowd in my mind. I want to apologize and ask them to stay.

How I wish I could.

But it's too late. Reflecting on the futility of any amend-making effort, I conclude that all I want to do is come inside, climb up to my room, and hide for the rest of my so-called vacation.

Pushing myself gruffly inside our home's welcome, dry heat, I place the milk on the counter and begin to slither, hopefully unnoticed, to my private quarters.

Dad stops me halfway up the stairs.

"Hey," he calls, "get down here. We need to talk."

I can't say there's much tension in our relationship, but I wish he would leave me alone.

I just want to get into the privacy of my room and sleep. Pretend that fateful night of two years ago never happened

Certainly, I tell myself, grades can't be in, already. I know I didn't do well on my Spanish exam, but certainly, I think, he will forgive me.

It's not as if he really hassles me that much about things anyway.

Even trying to assume something relatively mundane, like a low-average grade in a town where Spanish is useless, I have no desire to talk. Nonetheless, not wanting to pave the way to another argument, I slump down the stairs to endure the discussion.

I want to sit in the living room but, against my wishes, dad guides me into the kitchen where he has, I notice, hidden the milk in the refrigerator. I lean against a granite countertop and he, against the sink across from me.

Behind his head, the porch stares back at me. I wish he had waited until night, so that I didn't have to see, once more, that painful memory.

It's all there, in the setting sun – the garden, the patio, the fire pit.

But he can't read my mind. He crosses his arms and softens his face, looking at his feet.

"Is something wrong?" He asks. "You don't seem like yourself. At any other break, you'd be joking around with your friends. Hell, even at work, you're not as energetic as usual."

This sort of worry sounds strange, coming from my father. Usually all work and no play, he leaves little room for emotions and has never, since the night I shifted, asked me about my feelings.

He talked me down out of that state and helped me to shift back into human form. But if I had thought that this was going to precipitate him suddenly becoming a hands-on parent and suddenly reveal to me the mystery of how to shift effectively – well, I was disappointed.

Minimal is the best description of his parenting style.

While he has always accepted me being gay and has even encouraged me to embrace my shifter identity, he has never been one for affection. In fact, this marks the first time, in two and a half years, that he has noticed my lack of friends.

"Well?"

He raises an eyebrow when I fail to respond, persisting in a manner that tells me I must seem really off.

Knowing he would continue to pester me otherwise, I reveal everything. I tell my dad how, against his promises, no one has forgotten that fateful night.

I tell him how no one in this town takes me seriously anymore because I've come to be known as the weirdo who shifts whenever he gets turned on. And speaking of getting turned on, my love life is shit because who would want to be with someone who could literally kill them during sex? And, besides that, what man in this town likes men, too?

Dad stops me after the sex part, turning his head to the side and raising a hand before his face. I said he had accepted my sexuality, but that did not mean he was comfortable talking about his child's love life.

"Whoa, whoa," he says, "no need to get too personal, son. I have enough information to see what you mean. It's unfortunate that no one could put that incident behind them. When I was your age, we would've chalked it up to a bad trip. It must have something to do with the times..."

Oh, I tried that one, Dad, I thought.

I would have loved for my classmates to think this was the result of some bad pill that was doing the rounds. But unfortunately, no.

He trails off, face full of thought. I watch his eyebrows twitch slightly, and his eyes squint under the kitchen fluorescents.

After a pause, he cracks his knuckles and continues.

"Look, what I'm about to say may surprise you, but I don't know how to put it lightly. I can't make any promises, either, but I..." he trails. I can tell now he tries to organize his thoughts.

"...I have a former business partner who I think would be willing to work with you."

My breath hitches. Leaving Carlsbad, after this afternoon, sounds like something from a dream. Already, my mind turns in anticipation of a fresh start.

Dad clears his throat.

"This old coworker is, um, an interesting guy, to say the least, but I think he would appreciate your vision. He's in Chicago, so you'd have to finish your semester before going, but I think that would give you time to mull it over and for me," he rubs the back of his head, "to make arrangements."

I fight the urge to accept the proposal without thinking it over, and strain to avoid agreeing right away for, as dad told me, nothing is set-in-stone. And yet, or the first time in two years, I see a light at the end of the tunnel.

And to think, I thought myself satisfied with simply finishing my education and coming home. The prospect of escaping Carlsbad and starting life anew in Chicago churns my sluggish, depressed brain to life, in fact; I have a new will to live. With freedom knocking at my door, finishing the semester, as well as enduring the rest of break in Carlsbad, sounds less daunting.

Of course, I can't let my father see my enthusiasm. He has never favored expression, I reason, and such overt happiness after such a serious conversation would startle him.

Instead, I smile professionally, tell him his idea certainly sounds enticing, and approve his going forward with his plans.

In my room's private confines, I celebrate until, once again, I feel scales on my skin.

Chapter 6

Why are my customers so slow to change?

I've looked at three apartments this week, all of which still have that tacky, "Asian-inspired" mishmash of squares, lines, and glaring yellow from the early-2000s. If I hadn't known any better, I would have thought I was walking around in some backward town that took its interior design cues from last decade. I knew I was optimistic, thinking I would find better-quality clients in the information age.

My phone rings and, desperate to hear something other than my own internal bitch monologue, I answer.

A rich, relaxed accent nearly vibrates through the receiver.

"Hey, Storm. Remember me?"

Speaking of backward towns. Of course, I remember Ashton Marsh, the heat of his skin against my own, and the slightly musky smell of his hair product as I run my fingers through his thick, dark-brown locks.

The stirring in my gut affirms this memory, but it's only the middle of the day. I must remain professional, however, and deftly change the subject to something more neutral.

I ask dear Ashton if he's still doing fireplaces, and fail to resist the urge to ask whether his father, the formidable and staunchly-conservative Silus Marsh, has kicked the bucket.

Ashton replies in the affirmative. He has occupied the head of Marsh Home and Hearth on his own for the past fifteen years and he's calling about something related to his strangely-successful fireplace business.

I imagine Ashton will tell me about an article he read in some no-name publication, which expresses with absolute certainty that fireplaces will make a comeback in big cities.

Or, conversely, he will complain about how fire codes have finally hit his backward county, spiraling his business into financial despair. Other than my dealing in apartments and the fact that fireplaces go in apartments, I have no idea how the man could possibly draw a line between us.

Either way, as someone embittered at his leaving me all those years ago, I anticipate him begging me for a partnership to keep his current livelihood. I look forward to rekindling our old flame.

Different news comes from the other end of the line. Ashton says he's calling about his son, River, who has somehow hit twenty without me knowing about him. The young man intended to take over the family trade, but feels unwelcome in town, after a "mishap" two years ago.

I can only imagine what a "mishap" entails in a place like Carlsbad. Drinking one beer? Smoking one cigarette, or – God forbid – looking at one boy?

I suppress a chuckle, not wishing to offend my old thrall, but still, I ask: what was River's mishap, exactly, and why has it never resolved?

Ashton falls silent, then tells me, pointedly, that River shifted at his graduation party. The urgency in his voice catches my attention: having existed by his side throughout our school years, and having spent my childhood in Carlsbad, I know that small-town people rarely care about privacy. At this drastic shift in tone, I cannot formulate my shock.

Following a few more moments, I finally ascertain where the conversation will turn: shifting and dragons, all the things I conceal around my coworkers.

All vestiges of sarcastic impulse leave my mind. I am no longer in the mood for joking. I press the phone receiver tight to my ear and strive to turn the three deadbolt locks on my office door. I cup my mouth before whispering "yes" or, rather, a half-enthusiastic "maybe."

I listen intently as Ashton describes River, his son, to me. I hear how River knows he's a shifter, but how Ashton hasn't had the time to teach his son proper shifting technique. In the back of my mind, I wonder if Ashton did to River what his father did to him, ask him to guard a secret without understanding.

But Ashton never mentions his family.

He tells me that River's lack of experience in shifting leaves him vulnerable to fatal blunders. Two years ago, he clarifies River shifted in a heated moment of passion and alienated himself from the rest of the Carlsbad community.

He hasn't been the same since already at a loss due to his homosexuality. He rarely leaves his room, Ashton says, and is only out of the house at his request. In all, River has become a total outcast.

The story sounds much like my own, except River has the good fortune to live in a time when who he loves – at least, outside of Carlsbad – matters so much less than his shifter status. I feel mildly jealous that he does not have to endure the double-whammy that I experienced.

Ashton ends his – or rather, his son's – tale of woe by asking me if I would let River work under me.

I know better how River feels, Ashton explains, so surely, I would not mind taking River as an intern? He's in his third year of management studies, Ashton elaborates, so he could easily move to a higher position if he does well. River needs someone with a similar story to guide him.

As if the first half of the story weren't enough. I can already see myself adopting River as my own, and struggling to resist him if he has inherited – which I imagine he has – his father's beautiful blue eyes and clear, smooth, porcelain skin.

But, while I dream of his eyes physically, I already doubt his eye for design. Raised essentially to manage Marsh Home & Hearth, will he live up to my sharp taste?

Does he know how to furnish a modern home? This latter area is, I imagine, where he will need the most training.

I answer as I always have, with a mildly reluctant "maybe."

The boy will accept, I think, he, like me, will take any opportunity to get out of Carlsbad.

I'll get ready for a three-month – no, a six-month internship.

Even more time, I consider, admiring his beauty.

Chapter 7

A car howls past me, its horn sounding. Coming to a sudden halt in the tangle of rush-hour traffic, it splatters me with the dirty, puddle remnants of a late spring rain.

Sometimes I'm grateful, I think, that I left my car in Carlsbad. Rush hour looks like hell and, frankly, the trains give me everything I need.

The move, however, wasn't so smooth. Packing and planning required long telephone conversations, as well as frequent weekend trips home from school. The logistic madness of it all really put a damper on my studies and my social life, because you can neither work nor get drunk when learning your address, your rent, your salary, and the names of all the local pizza parlors.

Formulating strategies to avoid old classmates in Carlsbad also ate up my time, even though I rarely left the house during my returns. Furthermore, on weekend mornings, almost no one went looking for moving supplies. And, on the college end, I can't say I lost friends. I only grew more distant with those who knew nothing about my shifter status as the semester wore on.

Gazing at the endlessly tall gray buildings that surround me, I deem that what challenges and sacrifices I encountered leading up to the move were worth it.

Thanks to my boss, I have my own apartment. Sleek, modern, and in a central location, it is nicer than anything I could have imagined owning in Carlsbad. I also have no roommate, which means I can relish the peace, quiet, and privacy I feared I would miss by coming to the bustling metropolis.

I was dreading having to share with a stranger – this was one of the things that had worried me about going away to college in the first place.

Needless to say, I still hadn't gotten entirely comfortable in my ability to shift entirely when I wanted to or not. I didn't relish the prospect of some roommate walking in on me after an enthusiastic evening alone.

Because even in the depths of my imagination, I didn't dare hope that my life could ever contain anyone else.

Another perk is that I'm within walking distance of my office, as well as bars frequented by people of both the young and the gay variety. In the end, I have luxuries at my disposal that have never existed, in Carlsbad.

My boss, a mysterious man named Storm Woods, remains the only immediate thing – well, person – I have yet to discover in this spiraling city. Hopefully, I tell myself, he will live up to the expectation that I have carved into my head.

Chapter 8

I need not wait long for an appointment with Storm Woods, in his office, at his company's central Chicago location. Storm Woods has prioritized our meeting, so I hear because he plans to work with me one-on-one, unlike with most of his designers.

My dad told me that most of his crew wait months to get an interview, but my position comes sans portfolio: I'm an exclusive invitee to this domain.

Much of this information arrived via email, but I still find it daunting. Why would an interior design giant prioritize me, someone, who has never even owned a home, over someone who knows what they're doing?

Shifting constitutes my main reason for arrival, which makes the invitation stranger: could Storm Woods not just call me a troubled young adult?

I assume that my moving to the top of Storm Woods' list has something to do with him and my father's relationship, or whatever it is. If my father's ties to Storm Woods are what got me into the man's inner ring, then I'm no better than the sons of other, more successful and more coddling entrepreneurs. I haven't done anything to deserve my title. I've only taken advantage of my father's success and made no real progress of my own.

But then, I think, did I really want this job in the first place? I hadn't imagined working anywhere but Marsh Home and Hearth, although said prospect never incited much joy.

I remove my guilt from my mind and compose myself outside the office building. Flipping through my phone, I verify that I haven't, as I have many times, taken the bus in the wrong direction.

My phone buzzes to remind me that the interview begins in half an hour, which throws my mind again into a frenzy.

I work here, now, I affirm, to put myself at ease. I cannot be fired. This Storm Woods guy is a human, too. He was in my position, once, and was probably about my age when he was there. He has made mistakes, as I have, and will continue to make mistakes. He isn't perfect.

For the sake of mental stability, I will these thoughts to be true. Semiconsciously, however, I acknowledge that neither I nor Storm Woods are human; we're dragon shifters, and therefore probably the farthest from human one can go while still looking like a human. Perhaps we're all prone to human mistakes.

Besides, aside from the shifting, I don't know anything about Storm Woods. He may be perfect or, in more relatable terms, self-actualized. He may have inherited his fortune, needing no grueling interview process to become successful. He may have been born knowing how to choose a suit and tie.

I adjust my own tie without thinking, suddenly self-conscious that Storm Woods will find my outfit atrocious. I wonder if it's too formal, or if it betrays my small-town roots. What do people even wear to business meetings, I find myself asking, and is this an interview or a business meeting? What's the difference between interviews and business meetings? If I've never had an interview but have a job, what is this?

I edge into the skyscraper and pray for the best.

The building's interior seems to glitter. The fluorescent lights above shimmer off the black marble floor and the décor looks like a mix of modern business gray and avant-garde art deco.

"Mr. Woods will see you now," a blonde receptionist stands from behind a tall desk, calling me back to reality. Hot sparks of anxious fire have charged into my throat, and I will them back into my stomach. Shifting in this moment will doom me to eternal embarrassment.

The receptionist holds her trained gaze on me and, to her, I nod in affirmation. I am ready to face Storm Woods. The young woman steps out from behind her sleek, black barrier.

"Would you like me to show you to his office?"

I nod again.

She waves her hand cheerfully, "Follow me."

Chapter 9

The elevator ride to the three-digit floor does not last as long as I would have preferred. I feel the metal casement shoot me into the air, ascending at speeds that make my ears pop.

My surroundings lurch when I reach my destination. Stepping out of the elevator, I dizzily read the words printed on a tall set of doors: Storm Woods, Interior Designer. Finally assured I have made no misstep, I push my weight into the heavy closure.

"Ah, River Marsh. I've heard a lot about you!"

An endless space divides where I stand and where an impeccably-dressed man, who I assume is Storm Woods, reclines gracefully. I imagined that a space so large would have a waiting room or a coffee table, but Storm Woods does little to take the edge off his interviewees.

"Don't just stand there. Please – sit."

I step cautiously forward upon his command, cringing at the sound of my echoing footsteps on the uncarpeted floor.

In the dead-silent room, I am the only sound. The orange taste of fire leaps into my throat, for the second time today. I swallow.

I cannot become that nervous.

I cannot shift. I cannot shift, but I also cannot burn a hole in my esophagus.

I reach the desk after what feels like eons, pulling myself into a leather chair that nearly swallows me whole. The desk itself, carved of heavy wood and etched with intricate designs, stands two or three lengths longer and extends two or three lengths deeper than the average workspace. Two equally-formidable bookcases flank the structure, making the entirety of the ensemble not unlike a modern throne.

Storm Woods, dressed in tailored black, assesses me with a regal mien that merits no less than royal status. He possesses a slender build, with a chiseled skull perched atop a long, smooth neck. His eyes are somewhere between amber and orange in color, brought aflame by the rare bouts of the sun that grace the Chicago skies. He keeps his dark, long hair slicked back into a ponytail.

I study his upper body. Although slight upon the first impression, Storm Woods sports an undeniable amount of muscle. Something about his lean figure makes me want to reach forward and brush the tips of my fingers on his flesh, to sense the steamy warmth of his body beneath my skin.

He eyes my tie and clamps my fantasy short.

"I see you're not from around here."

My hands fly to my neck, and Storm Woods bursts into scathing laughter. His teeth gleam like fangs beneath the fluorescents that glow above us, and I can make out the pointed tip of his hot-pink tongue.

"Relax," he insists, waving his hand. "There are so many looks in Chicago, and so much more assuming than yours. You're wearing all black, so you blend right in. And besides," he kicks his feet onto his desk, "you're here for me to train you. It doesn't matter if you don't have the proper look right away; I would refine it, regardless."

"Training," I look at the floor. "Training in what, exactly?" I ask out of genuine curiosity, because dad never told me, specifically, if I would become an interior design intern, in practice.

And Storm Woods is no kinder.

"Refining," he answers, studying his nails. "You will learn how to conduct yourself better, and how to resent things well."

Not changing his position, he extends his long, right arm. I take his hand, the skin of his palm softer than I expected.

"I'm Storm Woods, by the way, in case you thought you had the wrong place. I specialize in urban interior design, although I'm looking to branch into other regions, as well. That is where I think you can help me."

I nod, assuming he will commence a conversation about fireplaces. The fact that he took an impossibly long time to introduce himself, and then turn my thoughts to the possible location of these "other regions" tells me he wants to get started. Before I can pose any question that would break his pace, however, my throat constricts. Something about Storm Woods bids me not to speak.

Storm Woods goes back to studying his nails.

"I realize that design isn't your main medium, but your reference left excellent word about your managerial skills. I plan to keep you behind the scenes initially, and perhaps take you into the field as soon as you evidence a sensitivity for color and pattern."

Storm Woods lowers his legs and bangs his hand on the table in an abrupt change of face,

"Color and pattern are foundations for the designing mind!"

Storm Woods centers himself, clearing his throat and adjusting his jacket.

"I intend to teach you something else, as well."

Finally, he takes his eyes from mine, scanning the room and relieving me of his terrifying stare. His gaze circles the room more than once before he leans within millimeters of my face:

"I wish to help you with dragon shifting. I'm a shifter myself and escaped a situation much like your own. Unlike you, I didn't have anywhere to turn. I want to make you successful not only in business but also in life."

The reveal, so sudden, leaves me speechless. What also takes my breath away, however, is how much I want to kiss the man I fear so intensely.

Chapter 10

Storm

River Marsh's eyes glimmer from across the room. Their color wavers between ice and cyan. His gaze looks like a sky glittered with emerald, like the green-tinted oceans of the Atlantic coast.

Yes, just as I suspected. He looks just like his father, or perhaps even more attractive. I become giddy at the thought.

Steady on Storm. I say to myself.

I endeavor to get my breathing under control. Otherwise, what kind of teacher am I going to be if I cannot even master my own impulses?

I invite River to take a seat, out of both politeness and my ability to smell his tightly-wound nerves. I want the boy to relax but, thanks to his sheltered upbringing around imbeciles who flinch at the slightest change, he lacks rapport with the dragon's senses. As such, he cannot possibly understand the message I send him. Even at twenty, he has not yet developed the mental and emotional acumen of the shifter breed.

River crosses the floor tentatively, as though he fears his steps will break the linoleum. I wonder, do the businesses in Carlsbad conduct their interviews threateningly? The look on River's face suggests the truth of my assumption but, more realistically, it also hints that daddy Marsh's status has prevented the boy from going to any sort of meeting.

River takes an hour's journey to reach me but finally curls into a chair, appearing petite when compared to the seat's large, plush, leather cushions.

Although he still retains some masculine features, he has inherited none of his father's brawn. I trace the lines of his slender, smooth thighs from beneath his new, department-store pants.

I imagine myself kissing those long stretches of skin, running my tongue into the crease of his hips as he trembles and begs me, to stop teasing him and take him into my mouth.

I see him succumbing to orgasm as my lips graze the tip and I hear myself gently reassuring him that soon, within an hour, we can try to go for longer.

I keep my eyes on his own oceans of blue to subdue the erection that yearns to leap forth, but God, I hope he feels my attraction. I hope he feels the strong hormonal signal I feel across the space that rests between us.

But now, I must stop fantasizing about his talent in the bedroom, and focus on the abilities that put him before me, at this moment. To create time for me to organize my thoughts, I begin with the obvious: His tie is too formal. He isn't from here.

River places his hands about his neck like he's about to strangle himself, but gives no real response. His eyes grow wider, forcing me to peer into them even more. Perhaps he's nervous.

Nervous. I laugh before I can stop myself, but then acknowledge that he is worlds apart from prior invitees. Having gotten wind of his history, agitating him too severely could bring a shift. As I rent my office space, I must avoid such an incident.

This young man sits in front of me, almost unable to look directly at me. As if he is scared.

This will never do and any unprecedented shifting is to be avoided at all costs.

I attempt to bring River out of shock but, as I cannot stifle my own sick sense of humor, it comes out half-assed. To my dismay, his embarrassed reaction to my – admittedly, inappropriate – behavior is precious.

The funny thing is that I haven't even got started yet. For me, this is respectable.

However, I know I should ease up here.

River is fragile. He is not one of my workaday conquests.

They belong in a different category altogether.

Before I give the wrong impression here completely, no, I don't go around propositioning just anyone nor acting inappropriately... with anyone who is not completely up for it.

My usual beaus are worldly wise if younger than me. There's never anything innocent about them.

Therefore, I must tread carefully. Not only has his father entrusted him to me – and this is enough of a reason to hesitate, but there is the whole might-burn-the-office-down with one wrong shift.

And if there ever was a reason to take it steadily, it was that.

Besides, just now, it wouldn't feel right until I had got him to relax.

His cheeks, once white, blush a magnificent candy-red color that would go succulently with my bed sheets. He's so demure, I notice, that I wonder what, exactly, ignites the passion that drives him to shift.

What prompted him last time, for example.

Probably some spotty youth.

And if that was the effect that some teenage waster could elicit that kind of a reaction, just think what someone like me could do.

I try and hide a smile at the pureness of this young man's looks. He is too demure at the moment for my liking.

Just now, it wouldn't be right.

Demure, yes, but brave enough to ask me why I have invited him. I'm not surprised, in truth, based on how his dad goes about things. The man probably gave only the basics on me, my profession, and my work.

I respond just as vaguely. Do I know how much I will insert him into the business? And, my sick and love-struck mind continues, how much he will insert himself into me?

Focus.

This sickness in my mind needs to be overcome.

I need to work at reaching out to the sealed off youth before me.

It is going to take a lot of time and a lot of work before he is even ready to interact with. In any way at all.

Like this, it just wouldn't be right in a million different ways.

So, I adopt a more casual tone, both to connect with him and keep my imagination at bay. I even go so far as to kick my legs onto my desk, risking damage to the enamel, to show just how casual I can be.

Still, however, I stick with the obvious: My name is Storm Woods, I'm an interior designer, I do mainly urban dwellings, but I want to move beyond that. I believe he, River, with his managerial skills and small-town experience, can help me get organized for said expansion and eventually help him in the field.

I feel relief wash over me. No mistakes on my end, but from him, no response. No affirmation. No signal of understanding. No questions. No complaints. Perhaps a nod, but a nod so subtle as to go unnoticed.

I take the silence as my cue to continue, but I curse inwardly at Ashton's failure to teach his son to vocalize.

Dialogue, I scream in my imagination, is what moves a meeting forward.

Do I really have to do all the talking here?

In the absence of any meaningful reply from River, I have to stop myself from making them up for him, in his voice.

It would be so easy to do, to take him off. His funny mannerisms. The way he melted into that chair and sat himself down in front of me.

His funny stilted way of speaking.

That rural Carlsbad drawl that they all have.

That I used to have until I taught myself better and made the decision to leave it behind. Leave them all behind.

Oh dear. I am verging back off into a fantasy again.

About River and his soft voice, washing over me.

It would be so easy to do. To let myself be seduced by this, but I must keep things formal. At least, in the beginning.

Instead, I focus down on what he is wearing. Frowning deeply, I realize that something must be done about this, at the very least.

It is unsatisfactory in the extreme.

Yes, River has no taste, and from his cheap suit and decision to wear a tie to a casual encounter, I can tell that he hasn't been to many executive business meetings.

I can see I am going to have to take him aside and show him a few things. About the types of social occasions and the appropriate clothing for each situation.

Has the boy even been on a date before? I wonder.

This thought pops into the center of my mind without warning. This is exactly the sort of thing I don't want to be thinking about, right now.

But it is an intriguing one. Silently, I wonder how he has gotten through the last twenty years without even an inkling of what clothes to wear and how to conduct oneself in any given scenario.

By the time I was his age I had begun already to make my way in the world.

I may have still been in college, but I was already branching out on my own in the world.

Beginning by gaining my first clients before I even graduated university.

Working on my own from the off, at least taught me a few things and one of those things was at least never to wear a cheap polyester suit to a meeting about interior design. Or anywhere, ever, preferably.

Chuckling to myself, I think, he has got a lot to learn. About everything, but firstly, I need to take him shopping and if necessary, put police tape all over the entrance to every department store in Chicago.

However, River's current inferiority is not – and shall never be – static to me. I know this is something that can and will change with time. And how much I want it to be.

This is what I mean by him not being ready, yet.

Given a bit of time and the right setting I know that this awkward young man is going to come to fruition in front of my eyes.

After all, he is twenty years old now. And hardly a child

But he will be, just not soon enough for my liking.

To get the ball rolling I start to try and connect once more with him. To get those flashing eyes to engage with me.

I want him to ask me questions, damn it, and I want him to stop me mid-sentence. I

want him to dominate me, both in the office and, I think salaciously, in the bedroom.

Eventually.

But yes. He could start by just fucking talking to me. For domination is the basis on which the shifter hierarchy functions.

A teacher is only of quality insomuch as his students can intellectually and physically overpower him, I repeat to myself the mantra from the Intro to Philosophy course I took in college. And looking at this pupil, I have a lot of work to do in at least one of these aspects.

But River, unable to hear my thoughts, continues his silence. I use the silence to my advantage, making a rather dramatic performance of our conversation about shifting.

I exaggerate my examination of the room, to ensure that no one will listen to this oh-so-confidential discussion.

I lean as close to my guest as possible, getting a whiff of a cologne so pungent as to signal to me his failure to use a dragon's sense of smell.

I tell him about my pedagogical mission quickly, to avoid devouring him hungrily from across my desk's large, wooden surface.

Looking over at his young face I see precisely nothing. Nada. Nil. Zero.

There is nothing there to show that anything that I have said or done or shown him in the past few minutes have made any mark on him at all.

This is unprecedented.

Once again, I find myself cursing Ashton for failing in his basic duty as a father so badly.

There is no connection there. No recognition of anything that I have been trying to demonstrate.

Surely, I think, my intensity would have driven him to feel something?

Still, however, I dismiss him without a word.

Chapter 11

River

When I think of Storm Woods, three adjectives come to mind: insanely attractive, dramatic as hell, and creepy as fuck.

This might be more than three adjectives, depending on what people think are adjectives. Either way, I sense that the man beats to his own drum in a highly-eccentric manner that, even in a place like Chicago, must terrify other people.

I can also tell Storm Woods is attracted to me. Since he sniffed me in our first meeting, I feel that our working relationship will be a shit storm of his straining with every fiber of his being not to push beyond professional boundaries, and my efforts to do the same.

Yes, I'm attracted to him, and that doesn't simplify the matter. He has some sort of spark that makes me want to drop everything and spend the rest of my life with him or, in more illicit terms, spend the rest of my days fucking him until he weeps. It may come from our being dragon shifters, I'm not sure, but there's some sort of connection that I would interpret as an attraction.

Nonetheless, if given the option to provide a totally anonymous appraisal of our meeting, I would say that Storm covered the basics well, but failed to give a definite answer about when it was okay to kiss him, when his schedule was open for more private forms of affection, and what the hell I'm doing here, in the first place.

Yet, there is something inherently unsettling about being attracted to a man your father's age.

This is the one thing that is stopping me and holding me up from even thinking about making my fantasy a reality.

How do you justify wanting someone who's decades older than you, and may have only a few more years to function properly? According to what I've learned about natural selection in high school and college, this sort of attraction doesn't follow any natural law.

Thankfully, spending the evening masturbating in my apartment does not give me time to ponder Darwinism.

With my hand wrapped around my painfully erect member, I imagine myself prostrating below the older gentleman, and bending to his eccentric – and probably highly-erotic – will. I imagine him using his control of dragon shifting to ravish me. He burns me with his fiery breath and whispers sweet nothings in his ancient tongue. I try to answer back but to no avail. Despite his teachings, he remains superior to me.

In the grip of fantasy, I feel grateful that my job has provided me with someone so incredibly intoxicating. This is the first time I've entertained having a potentially consistent sexual partner, and perhaps a lover if our feelings align. I take the possibility as an added perk.

My hips jolt and I spill over my hand and brand-new office chair. Coming down from the masturbatory high, I consider that the professional atmosphere will put a damper on our love life if that is indeed what this internship becomes.

It seems crazy that I have already begun to think of him in these terms.

We will have to restrain ourselves for multiple hours per day – perhaps without reprieve – before a crowd that will only grow denser as I move into the field.

At just twenty, I can taste the scandalous office life that some people don't describe until thirty or forty.

With more time before me and less experience behind me, how will I handle my desires?

More importantly, as Storm Woods is the CEO, how will he handle his attraction to me? How will it affect my shifting – our shifting – if we ever reach that point?

In all honesty, I am not sure what even consenting dragons do together, once the scales come out.,

Despite the shining street lamp outside my window, the darkness of my room and the relative silence of the cars alert me to the time. Glancing at the digital clock to my right, I see that only hours separate me from my first full workday.

Standing, legs still shaky from sexual release, I thumb through my closet and select an outfit that I surmise Storm Woods will find up-to-code. Even if still sub-par, it is far superior to today's number.

I don't bother to brush my teeth, changing into my pajamas, I check my arms and legs for any scales that may have seen my carnal bliss as a chance to rear their ugly heads.

Chapter 12

I sit under the lonely light of my kitchen table, an old-fashioned pen-and-paper set in-hand. It is getting late and the noises of the day have subsided.

This is usually the time of day that inspiration comes to me and when I can get some serious thinking done.

All day long in my office I am supposed to be creative and come up with ideas and designs for the tasteless citizens of Chicago. However, usually, I find that in the rush of the daytime, with the never-ending ringing of the telephone and constant interruptions, actually getting some work done is best left to this time of the day.

In other words, night time.

Living with the noise of the world and in particular other humans, is one of my bugbears. It is impossible to be creative or even formulate any ideas at all with all their sound.

And now, I have got one more distraction; River.

If I thought it was hard before working in the office with everything that was going on, it was nothing on the distraction that River has brought.

Of course, he is completely oblivious to the effect that he is having on me. Just his mere presence in the room throws me off kilter.

Why does he have to stand there looking so damned sexy?

Take earlier, when he was there, bundled into my oversize leather chair. I had never noticed that it was oversized before it had his diminutive frame in it. Now it looks too large. Too large for him and too large for that room.

How come I had never noticed before? Some interior designer I am.

Work has been piling up and up on my desk, that I simply have not been able to get through because of this issue. Every time I try and concentrate, I close my eyes and there he is. The vision of River Marsh appears and refuses to fade.

In my mind, he is far more daring than the real version who fidgets nervously in front of me.

The River who lives in my imagination is much more lively and quick to take charge of the situation. To take charge of me.

Those blue eyes which glow with a light of their own. They power through my daydreams and stop me from working anywhere, no matter what the time of day is.

I sigh again. Because even in the peace of the still evening that surrounds me, I am still being persecuted by the vision of River occupies my mind.

But this time, I am not attempting to work. I have given up with that for the moment, to try something even more impossible.

That of trying to work out what the hell to do with River.

And here, by what to do with I mean professionally and well, from a tutorial point of view.

What to do with River in every other respect is something that I can barely keep out of my fevered imagination.

No, what I need to do now is to start his transition from random dragon shifting, to something confident, assured and under control.

Once again, I scratch my head and wonder how it is that Ashton has managed to bring a child to adulthood, without ever once giving him any type of tuition in this matter.

Even my father, who was never going to win awards for his parenting, had managed to reluctantly show me the basics.

The memory of his terse commands and general bad-tempered instruction still linger with me. All the same, he got the job done.

I like to think that I was also a bit more fucking pro-active than either River or his father in the whole business of shifting.

I mean, I know it's not easy, but alternatively, it is also not rocket science and can be picked up with a bit of instinctive fine tuning.

But instinct is something that I can see precious little of in River, so far.

Which is why I am stuck here at stupid o clock in the evening, still searching for some inspiration.

I stare down at the page in front of me. I have got nowhere since I began this charade exactly two hours ago.

At the top of the page sits the word plan, written in capital letters and underlined for emphasis. I pen tomorrow's date in the paper's top-right corner. Despite ruminating in silence for almost two hours, nothing comes to me.

Typical. Inspiration only comes when it isn't obligation. In any other scenario, I could easily coax someone as young and attractive as River into the woods for some fun.

As soon as this idea has presented itself to me, it has fixated itself firmly into my head and refuses to budge.

River.

...In the woods...

I can hardly stop thinking about it and it is distracting me from concentrating on the task at hand once more.

The dragon thing doesn't help. River knows and I know, as well, yet something within me warns that, if I approach the situation too quickly, the boy will flee and all will be lost.

I have spent most of our time together tiptoeing around him.

The last thing I want to do is either scare him or produce a reaction in him that leads to another unwitting transition.

I mean, apart from anything else, there are people around us all day long.

I really can't risk something like that from happening.

No, we must go somewhere that it is safe.

But where?

And what could the pretext possibly be?

He appeared so timid in our meetings – what would work? I place my head in my hands. How do you connect with someone so closed-off?

I stare at the phone, which blinks on its charger across the room. Maybe calling Ashton wouldn't hurt.

But calling Ashton would also mean admitting that I didn't listen to him as closely as I should have. Heaven knows, he was jabbering on for long enough.

Calling Ashton would mean asking for help, a task my pride won't allow. Calling Ashton would mean hiding the enthusiasm I have for working with his son who, if anything, has inherited his slightly plain, but nonetheless seductive good looks.

He has entrusted this boy to me and won't be suspecting anything.

Idly I wonder if he will be as uptight as his father proved to be. Certainly, the first impressions that he has given me would seem to say so.

Damn!

Now I have the unwelcome visitation of Ashton in my mind as well.

And he was hard work too. Hard work which inevitably came to nothing.

How I was hoping that River would prove less intransigent than his father was in succumbing to my charms.

It might have been more than twenty years ago, but this still forms a substantial body blow to my pride.

To cut a long story short, I am not used to being turned down and I am accustomed to getting my own way.

I have never had any complaints from any other quarters.

Naturally, River is not the only young man occupying my mind. Well, occupying my time anyway, but he is the one who is above and away in the lead of my imagination there.

There are one or two others as well. But none of them have captivated my imagination in the same way as he has.

I knew he would.

As soon as Ashton mentioned that he had a son, I couldn't help wondering what he was like.

And as it turns out, he is no carbon copy of his father, but just with enough of the same elements to make him interesting. Even more interesting, maybe.

Speaking of Ashton, I cast my mind back and try hard to think. Just what did he say to me all that time he was on the phone for? I try to think but just can't. I was too busy ruminating on the fact that he had a son in the first place.

I guess his father had done what he said he was going to do, all those years ago, when he swore Ashton off me. He said he was going to get him straightened out and I suppose he did.

It didn't surprise me that Ashton had so obediently followed the will of his father. He had always been a slave to duty. Whatever it was that we had had, or, what I had thought we had had, well it just faded away.

If I am being honest, he never felt the same pull to me as I did to him. But this time, I am resolved that history would not repeat itself.

These things were stopping me from picking up the phone and making that call.

There was in effect a hell of a lot of reasons why I didn't want to have to call Ashton about anything, least of all, about how best to connect with his son.

So, I turn my attention back to the paper.

I tear through the sheet.

I think I am trying too hard here to impress. Dreaming up complicated programs designed to look like bona fide "training".

Perhaps simple honesty would work. The boy saw my unpredictable side during our first meeting, and he saw my dramatic suspicion regarding others' knowing our secret.

But this rendezvous should also look like business, I remind myself.

Like Ashton, my career will fall into the gutter – or maybe onto tabloid headlines – if I reveal my identity.

It is obvious that I cannot conduct our business, or indeed any kind of business with River in the office.

Home isn't really any better for much the same reasons.

I don't really harbor any desire to turn my study into dust by an inexperienced bout of fire-breathing.

Certainly, I don't relish the prospect of the place being reduced to ash – in fact, I don't even want to risk the possibility of a solitary burn mark on any of my genuine Queen Anne furniture. Not a chance baby.

I'm going to have to take him somewhere else. But where?

All the usual places, my normal haunts, where I would go with young men – either of the dragon variety or otherwise – well, they just aren't going to cut it for all the same reasons that home or the office will not.

The problem is that River is an unknown quantity. A variable. A big question mark. I don't know what the hell he is going to be capable of or not, we can't be out anywhere in public if it all goes wrong and that pretty much rules out most of the city of Chicago.

I look at the clock. It's nearly midnight, and still, I have no idea. Tired and out of options, I note down words on the sheet, hoping to make associations until I can write something of coherence.

Woods

Dragon

Naked

Gay

Sex

Eyes – God, those eyes.

Forest

Alone

Together

Camping

Camping. That's it. We're going camping.

Now – to make camping something interior designers normally do.

Business

Work

Meeting

Private

A private business meeting while camping?

I put the pen down, imagining how ridiculous everything will sound. However, for lack of ideas, it will have to do.

The boy may find something intriguing, I imagine, about a company whose higher-ups take time away from the city.

Given his country background, he may find something attractive – dare I say sexy? – about living among nature.

At least I am hoping so.

They have got to have some pastimes still in Carlsbad, haven't they?

Casting my mind back, I seem to recall endless hazy summers of camping, hunting and other far too wholesome pursuits being relentlessly shoved down the throats of us young boys.

Things can't have changed that much can they?

Leaving the pen and paper on the table, I finally retire to bed.

Thank God for that. I think, drifting off to sleep.

We're going camping. That should be nice and easy, shouldn't it?

In the night, I imagine the boy standing over me, dominating me as I pray, one day, he will be able.

When this might possibly happen is not something that I can excite myself with just yet.

We must get through the basics first.

And there's a hell of a lot of ground to cover there.

The spot I am thinking of taking him to will be calm and tranquil and as near as possible to deserted.

As I fantasize about the upcoming trip, about him, things all come to a head inside of me.

Yes. He's there. His cyan eyes shining like celestial bodies through the dark of the trees.

There will be a secluded spot, a clearing, somewhere in the forest.

There's going to need to be because I don't want any amateur attempts at fire-breathing resulting in the first forest fire to hit Chicago for God knows how long.

And talking of fire... the impression of River, leaning over me and staring, with those big sparkling, surprising jewels of his. It is raising my temperature. In all sorts of ways.

Damn!

Lying there, between my orange satin sheets I realize I am going to have to unburden myself.

Fire rises in my own body as I bring myself to a hot, heavy-breathing state of release.

Chapter 13

River

"I need you in my office, pronto," Storm Woods commands, his eyes peeled. His gaze is more orange than usual, today, and he appears livelier than before. Combined, these traits make me, for some reason, more fearful.

I follow him into his large office, hearing the door slam behind us as we move, Storm himself striding lightning-fast, to the desk surrounded by leather chairs.

I plant myself exactly where I sat, the day prior. Storm takes his place in his director's chair, crossing his legs instead of stretching them on the varnished surface.

The man pulls a pad of paper, emblazoned with illegible messy handwriting, from his desk drawer.

"I'm going to tell you everything you need to know about your internship," he begins, his voice low. "I don't know who's listening, so don't ask questions and don't mention dragons."

He punctuates that last three words, eliciting from me a nervous nod.

"The higher-ups go on outings every so often," he starts the phrase as though it belongs in any normal conversation. "We have a camping spot rented in at Lake Isle Park, which is north of here. As our intern, we want you to be a part of these excursions."

He winks, alerting me to the fact that his words contain a hidden message. I simply nod, to signal both that I understand what he says, and that I know to infer what he means.

"Anyway, we make little training sessions out of these outings and look for inspiration in the woods. They tend to be more productive than relaxing, but it does get us out of the city for a while. I'm telling you this because we're going on one next weekend, and I want you to be prepared."

I nod again. From what I have gathered, Storm and I are not the only shifters, here. There are others, too, who get training from their CEO.

There has been one other guy, an older man, around the same age as both Storm and my dad. Called Silverton, or something.

He has made himself known to me, in strange, half-formed surreptitious glances.

I tried to open a conversation with him.

It went something like this;

"Um. Are you one of Storm's trainees?"

I had emphasized the word trainee as some sort of dragon code. I wasn't sure whether he was one of the shifters that Storm had mentioned or not but thought that there had to be some reason for the guy's continued creepy looks over to me in the staff canteen.

"No"

And with that, he walked away from me, at pace.

So, that concluded my one and only attempt to break into the inner circle of shifting at Woods Interior Design HQ. If even such a thing existed in the first place.

All in all, I hadn't seen an awful lot of evidence of a dragon shifting community at work.

Perhaps I would be better off keeping quiet about this sort of thing in future.

Back in the office, I shake myself a little to realize that Storm is still addressing me and more than that, looking as if he expects some sort of response, too.

He is there, staring at me as if he has just asked me something and for the life of me, I am not quite sure what it was.

"Well?" he says keenly.

I have absolutely no idea what to say to him.

"Um," I say, hesitantly.

Storm breaks his businesslike tone and leans forward onto his desk.

"You have gone camping before, haven't you?"

I gulp. In all honesty, I'm not one for the great outdoors.

Even in Carlsbad, where no building or house went without the view of a cornfield or forest, I never felt inclined to embrace the wilderness; I contented myself with admiring nature from afar.

Some of this might have been because perhaps it was all around us, I never really felt the need to go exploring it.

Boy scouts and all those outdoor types of bores never really appealed to me.

Storm's face falls flat as though, once again, he has read my thoughts.

"Don't tell me," he says, deadpan, "your dad was too busy to do that, too."

The conversation begins to take the same tone as yesterday's, only with Storm placing more obvious emphasis on his thoughts about my father. He feels disappointed, I can see, in my dad and myself. He visibly assumes that my dad failed to raise me, and has enlisted an old colleague to take over the job.

I jump to defend against that notion.

"No, no, it's not what it looks like. Yes, my dad never took me camping, but it wasn't because he didn't want to. I didn't want to go outside. I've never wanted to go camping."

Storm huffs;

"So, you've never been a true citizen of Carlsbad, then?"

I shrug. If anything, the statement offers a hint of understanding.

"Yes," I nod, "I never liked going outside when I was little, and I can't say things have changed. If that's what makes a citizen of Carlsbad, then I can tell you I've never been one."

Storm huffs again.

"Okay, okay, that's totally fine. I'll admit that we're not much for getting down and dirty, either. It's only a few times a month, and it's a time to disconnect. I think you'll enjoy it regardless."

He removes his gaze from mine and stares blankly at his desk. A hopeless look touches his expression, and the color fades from his cheeks.

I want to ask what's wrong, but am unable to believe in my own ability to articulate.

"So," I ask instead, "what else do I need to know about the internship?"

"Oh, right," Storm snaps out of his reverie and thumbs through a file. "I've decided to put you on the financing end. You're a business major, am I right?"

I nod in the affirmative, feeling my body relax. Storm does have a human side, which he cleverly hid during our first encounter. I silently regret that it didn't show yesterday for, maybe then, I would have had a chance to express myself to him.

Storm hands me a pile of papers.

"Here is our company manual. I expect you to work forty hours a week, and you will receive compensation for outings and meetings. Dress code is," he waves his hand before his face, "something more casual and less hideous than what you're wearing, now."

I nod again and stand, taking the manual as my cue to leave. Storm does not oppose to my awkwardly edging out the door.

Chapter 14

Storm

Stupid. Stupid, stupid, stupid!

The child only vaguely knows the extent of his dragon powers but has already blocked my capacity for seduction.

Or maybe, I think humbly, I'm too seduced, myself.

But my silent, empty office reeks of massive failure. Why, after yesterday's successful show, can I now do nothing graceful before the boy?

I just didn't get anywhere with him at all today.

So, he hates the idea of going camping. Well, that's just great. What am I going to do now?

In the absence of any better ideas, I guess I am just going to have to plow ahead regardless.

I chalk it up to lack of preparation. It is my fault I guess though.

I should have analyzed him more, rather than focusing on my body's response to whatever dragon signal he – probably unknowingly – sent at our first meeting.

I should have kept in better touch with Ashton, as much as I would have hated to do so.

Yeah. It would have hurt but despite everything that happened between us – or didn't – he was my best friend from home and cutting him out of my life completely scarred me more than I liked to admit.

At least then I would have known that he and whats-her-name had a kid. That sort of knowledge might have been handy over the last two decades or so.

It might have given us the excuse to bring the strands of our friendship back together after everything had blown apart.

This was hard for me to realize, but I had missed Ashton over the intervening years and I wondered if he missed me too.

Don't get me wrong, I wasn't alone. I rarely had the opportunity to be lonely. But in terms of a real friend to talk to about... stuff. There wasn't anyone, not really.

And by the fact that Ashton had just called me up, after twenty years, to ask a favor about a son I had previously no knowledge of, he didn't have anyone else in his life either.

I suppose I had been put off by old man Marsh.

The way he spoke to me, to us, forbade Ashton from having anything to ever do with me again.

It wasn't that he had been a stuck up pompous asshole about us. It wasn't the fact the man was a bigoted homophobic bastard of the worst type. It wasn't that which hurt. It was the fact that Ashton listened to him.

Listened to him over listening to me, or even, himself.

Of course, in my inner thoughts, I have decided that this wasn't really what he wanted for himself. That if he had been given a free choice and free reign over his life back then, that he would have chosen me.

Maybe that sounds conceited, but it's the way it works best in my mind. I don't know if it is really true.

Part of me can't help but think that if Ashton had truly thought as much of me as I did of him back then, that he wouldn't have been so easily swayed about what his damned father thought.

The disappointment of something that happened over twenty years ago still burns deep inside me.

It was a wound that would not completely heal. The pride, that is.

I like to think that I had gotten over Ashton years ago.

But now, here, with his magnificent young son sent in his stead to tempt me. I don't know.

The thoughts cloud my head about how I should proceed and how I should respond to this reluctant young man who has now become both my charge and also my potential lover all in one confusing phone call.

I cast my mind back to our less than productive meeting.

I think that I could have handled things better.

For a start off, I should have demanded the young man answer when I speak to him – that is what the Carlsbad folks would do if their ways haven't changed since my departure.

No way should I have let him gaze at his feet, at the floor, at the sky outside in the window behind me... in short, just anywhere other than my eyes.

Fancy getting to twenty years of age and having no idea on how to conduct oneself in company. Company of any description – not even just the formality of a business meeting. This boy doesn't know how to handle a one to one situation.

God knows what sort of a manager he is going to make if he can't do that one simple thing.

There is so much to teach him, I don't know where I am going to begin.

I could analyze the situation all day, but business orders me to move on. I'm looking at a house today, of all things, a little Victorian place on the wealthy end of town. The owner wants to capitalize on the place's "character" which, from my experience, means they want lots of brocade and lots of bohemian charm.

Oh yes, and there's also the restaurant, a grill looking for a way to stay in-tune with their "flame-seared" theme.

I have – perhaps foolishly – agreed to take River with me. To see how a 'real' business meeting is conducted.

And my eyes are already rolling at the outfit that he has chosen to wear. Maybe not quite as much polyester as yesterday's effort, but all the same, enough static electricity in it to power that restaurant's God-awful neon sign, that the owner insists on keeping.

Already, I am wondering how I am going to balance dealing with the garish tastes of the owner and directing River's bouts of fidgety nerves, both at the same time.

How wonderful, I think, that I will have to face the reality of shifting, and therefore the reality of River, all day.

As well try and fend off some real tat being installed around me.

And on top of that, I must invest in some real camping gear. I doubt River will trust a man who goes without a tent, or an R.V., or whatever non-outdoorsy outdoors people use when they're not dragon shifters.

There isn't much time to do any of this in, either, if we are to start our first lesson by the weekend.

In the same vein, I pray that someday, he will appreciate the added privacy.

And talking of privacy, out of my desk I bring a notepad, one that has been well thumbed through over the years.

I guess you could call it a journal.

It's not like I even fill it out anymore. But I used to do.

Back in the old days, I used to cover each square inch with the feverish intimate details of our every acquaintance.

And then, when there wasn't anything to report, I'd simply daydream and write what my crazed imagination would come up with.

Just for a moment, I open the book and it falls open at a particularly verbose chapter from over twenty years ago.

The handwriting is small and spidery. That hasn't changed too much. Even to myself, I find it hard to read it back.

"Down at the brook today, it happened again. We were sitting there fishing when suddenly, the transformation was upon me... the fire and the burning just got too intense. The only way out of this horror was to leap into the stream, completely naked.

The way he looked at me..."

I close the book abruptly. I cannot bear to get to the end of it.

The memory of that afternoon in the brook. Me and Ashton, skinny dipping. Trying to fight it. Trying to stop myself from shifting there and then, in his presence.

And why?

A question I have asked myself over and over?

Ashton should have been the one person it was alright for me to reveal myself to in that form. Why should he have been scared off by seeing me shift?

But like River, I didn't want him to know the strength of my feeling. I didn't want it to be obvious that I was out of control around him.

Just the same as his son's present-day mishap, I had already suffered a misfortune in public and once was enough – even in the presence of another shifter.

The fact was, that for shifters, neither Ashton nor his ramrod straight father Silus, were very keen on... shifting.

They both seemed to act as if it were something shameful. Any sort of acknowledgment of emotion was highly problematic to the pair of them.

The prospect of me shifting and turning all scaly again on Ashton, therefore, filled me with dread.

It's not that Ashton couldn't or wouldn't shift. He was just in perfect control over his every sense. There was no danger of him being struck down by an accidental erection that threatened to blow everything out of the water, quite literally.

No danger of him being a slave to his emotions.

Ashton was always in command of every situation and that absolutely included his shifting.

No wonder he had assumed that his offspring might have inherited the same steely disposition.

But I see something else in River's eyes.

Now I know it...

I haven't been having all these disquieting feelings about him because he is Ashton's son and heir. It is not because he reminds me of his father that I find him so irresistibly attractive…

It's actually because he is nothing like him.

Nothing like him in temperament.

If there is one thing I have gleaned about River thus far it is that he is a slave to his emotions as much as I am.

He just hasn't learned how to harness them yet.

And the thing that was worrying me so much and making me retreat, take a step backward about him – that he was simply a replacement for his father.

Well, now I know that this is not true.

I don't like River because he is the same as Ashton. It's because he is the same as me.

Him and I have a damn site more in common than Ashton Marsh.

The revelation of this fact comes as a blessed relief to me.

I'm not simply transferring my feelings in some horribly gauche sort of way from one generation to the other.

Thank God.

Because the thought of being like some old creep was really starting to get to me.

I have recognized something in River that I was not expecting to find.

Maybe I had been expecting a physical attraction and for it to be left at that, but there is more to it than that.

This could be a meeting of the minds, between us.

River Marsh has the latent talent to be a very powerful dragon, he just doesn't know it yet.

It's up to me to bring it out.

And for that, he is going to need some space to work it out in.

A glance downward shows me that I, too, require space. How pathetic that even my thinking about the boy results in this type of reaction.

Pressing a button on my office phone, I call my secretary to set things in order.

Chapter 15

River

Storm's office. It's the second day of my internship.

I am still not completely sure how my first day went.

Storm took me to a couple of his clients and I wasn't certain what I was supposed to bring to the meeting.

Other than rolling his eyes at my clothing, he didn't offer very many pointers, much less any actual training whilst we were there.

And Storm did his level best to ignore me the entire time we were out.

Settling in back at the office wasn't really any better either.

The accounts were easy enough to knock into shape. Besides that, I wasn't too sure what I was supposed to be doing on a day to day basis.

I found myself hanging around the office like a bad smell. In between clients' visits and bookkeeping, there wasn't as much to do as I would have liked.

One particularly tedious morning I was sitting with the accounts, scrutinizing a transaction, when one of the managers, Silverton, entered, with a sly look on his face.

"So, you off to the hills this weekend sweetie," he said with a wink that both alarmed me and knocked me off kilter.

Seeing the effect that he had had on me, the man looked even more smugly pleased with himself.

Silverton Wolf was approximately fifty years of age. Maybe a little older than my father. I am not sure as to whether he was the same age as Storm.

I couldn't even be certain what age Storm was or if he even had one. It was hard to imagine him being born at all, let alone being a child or youth. Someone like him must just have had to... evolve... fully formed.

Silverton smiled at me again, a smile I didn't fully trust.

It was like he hadn't stopped laughing at me since the moment I crossed the threshold to Woods Interior Solutions.

"Yeah. Um. You …coming?" I asked nervously.

I think I must have forgotten his complete dismissal of this matter the last time I asked him. I soon remembered.

"No sweetie. Some of us don't need any training"

And with that, he gave me a knowing wink and was about to turn to walk out of the room. It seemed as if he had only come in to taunt me.

But then he stopped. His trademark silver gray hair hanging down around his face. He turned on his perfectly groomed heel and returned to my gaze.

"Oh. Wow. Yes. I can see the resemblance"

Silverton continued walking up to me, staring at me as if I was some sort of exhibit or curiosity.

"Yes. I can see it now. Are you Ashton's kid? That's right?"

"Um. Yes. You know my dad?" I asked.

There was something about the superior look he gave me that made me instinctively want to ram his glistening teeth down his throat.

He didn't answer my question, but just raised his eyebrows and said;

"Pale imitation though kid. It won't last"

What the fuck was the creepy old asshole on about?

"Pardon," I said formally, my ire beginning to show.

"His interest. It won't last. You're not in his league at all"

And with that, the old queen sauntered out of the room.

Chapter 16

Ashton

I wasn't expecting to hear from River so soon after his last phone call.

He didn't call that frequently from college – not even the first week he had attended.

So, I was rather surprised that he called me not only on his first night, after safe arrival, as I had asked him to, but also on the second and then subsequent night after.

"Who is Silverton Wolf?" he said, without any preamble or pretense at asking after me or the fortunes of Marsh Home and Hearth.

"Um, who"

"Silverton Wolf" he repeated.

I thought I could detect a tension in his voice.

Silverton Wolf.

I ran the name through my memory banks. It resonated with me from somewhere but I wasn't entirely sure where from.

It didn't sound completely right.

"You... mean... Silver...Silver Fox?"

"Silver Fox?"

"Yeah," I said. "Tall, slim, about 6 feet 2. Lank silver hair down to his shoulders. Cowboy boots"

"Cowboy boots?"

River's voice bounced off the phone line. I could practically see him squinting in thought down the line.

"I was with you till the cowboy boots," he said. "But the rest of the description fits. Cowboy boots? You sure?"

The vision of Storm I had in my mind would have no truck with something as tacky as cowboy boots, I suppose. Which might explain things.

"Yeah. Corny, right? Even for Carlsbad" I laughed down the line.

"There's no way Storm would ever permit it," he said, but he was deadly serious.

"Well, I'm guessing that Storm has dressed the wily old goat up in his own image since we last met. Yeah. Silver was one of his interior designers. I'm guessing he's still on the scene then?"

"I guess so. How does he know you Dad?"

River seemed to be determined to ask a lot of questions today that just didn't make sense.

I thought for a moment before giving my answer.

"I... don't know. I just know that he was one of Storm's top designers..."

"Would you say that they were... closer than that?" He asked.

"Maybe," I said, not quite getting to grips with the turn of his questioning.

"They're definitely friends – oh!"

Then, the penny finally dropped.

He was asking me if Storm and Silver were lovers. I expect they probably were.

But whether they still are, nearly twenty years later, I just could not say.

"If you mean is he his boyfriend? Then, you're best off asking him"

"No, I..."

Now I can sense him backtracking.

I am wondering why he is so full of questions about Storm suddenly. I suppose it could be natural curiosity and nothing more.

And Silver is a pretty formidable character in his own right. Never mind when he is teamed up with someone like Storm.

I can imagine the combination of an office environment, with both Silver and Storm at the helm, being a daunting one for a nervous young kid like River.

I wonder pensively if I have done the right thing in sending him to work there.

"Are you okay there, River?"

"Yes, yes, I'm fine. I just wanted to know that's all" he said, shutting both me and the conversation down flat.

He doesn't stay on the line long after that. In fact, I haven't even managed to find out if he has made any progress with his shifts yet.

It doesn't seem like something that he wants to discuss.

I hang up, slightly unsure.

I guess I am going to have to trust Storm and whatever methods he chooses to employ to teach River about being a successful dragon shifter.

It certainly can't be any worse than my completely non-existent techniques.

The thing is, I don't ever recall needing that many pointers to work out the basics.

Not that I am blaming River.

Maybe it helped that I had Storm.

Another person my age, with whom we could learn together.

It occurs to me now that River has never had that.

Not only have I been completely neglectful in the whole area of his 'dragon studies' but I also haven't put him in touch with anyone in his age group who can help.

Now, I have been left at the mercy of asking the only person that I could think of to get help from – Storm.

I fight the temptation to pick up the phone and demand of Storm exactly what it is that he is planning on doing to help River but realize this would be completely out of order.

And deep in my mind, River's question has now seeded itself. I can't help wonder what is the nature of Storm's relationship with Silverton, after all this time.

Then I stop and laugh at myself.

Storm would love that. They both would.

It would appeal to Storm's ego no end, if he thought I was ruminating about the state, or otherwise, of his relationship.

Silver had always been on the horizon back then when I knew Storm better.

He came on the scene when he went away to college.

And he made it clear that he wanted me out of the way so that things could just be him and Storm.

Not that there ever was any me and Storm.

As far as I was concerned.

Not really.

Chapter 17

For relocating to the city, we certainly spend a lot of time in the wilderness. Every weekend, Storm packs himself and me up for a weekend alone, in the winding forests that separate Chicago from Wisconsin and Minnesota.

Oh, and about the alone thing, they are never – and never were – business trips.

Storm's team stared at me like deer in headlights when I mentioned his proposal, and told me frankly that the man probably did that stuff on his own time.

Silverton had made it clear enough that it was just going to be me and Storm.

Although, I still can't glean from the looks he was giving me whether this was something that met with his approval or not.

I hadn't seen or spoken to him since our paths crossed back at the office, a few weeks ago.

But as for being alone with Storm, well, that is going to take some getting used to.

Seeing as how dragon shifters only can shift "on their own time," these solo excursions come as no surprise. Storm calls these trips a "search for inspiration," but I, enduring the brunt of Storm's strictness, call them intense dragon shifter training sessions.

I'm not sure if maybe Storm thinks he is also there to answer the call of the wild, seek some divine intervention or come up with the color scheme for his latest open plan living collection, but I don't think that it's come to fruition for him.

What he is getting out of these sessions, so far, it is hard to tell. He's not showing whether this is strictly business or pleasure for him. Or maybe a combination of both those things.

Does he resent spending all this time with me, like this?

Have I been a disappointment? I can't help but think so, so far, anyway.

I know he is attracted to me. I can sense it, sometimes, in his eyes. But as of yet, he hasn't indicated it to me.

As much as Storm Woods infuriates and irritates, the attraction is mutual. But at the same time, there exists a raging mutual antipathy between us.

Not that it shows.

On the surface, that is, anyway.

It's not as if we ever argue, about anything.

To a casual observer, we had the perfect, if stiffly formal, relationship. For a boss and an intern.

Or even, for a pupil and a teacher.

If it is one thing that I have noticed about Storm is it is that he is determined to succeed at what he does.

Obviously, in the world of interior design, that box is already ticked.

He is something of a celebrity in his field and as I have now had impressed on me numerous times (yes, especially by Storm himself) that kids my age are queuing up around the block to intern for him.

Several of his staff I suspect, have looked at me with disdain for lacking the necessary qualifications to come and work here at Woods Interior Solutions.

Silverton is just the leader in the field of the disparaging looks and sharp comments.

But anyway, Storm likes to do things properly and this includes on taking on the mantle of teacher.

He does not give up, although I am not sure I would rate his technique all that highly, it does seem to have at least broken through the absolute basics.

Not that he gives any praise. Never.

So, I don't yet feel confident, but he is pressing on regardless.

Shifting is the only thing we've mastered. Storm Woods blames my slow progress on mere incompetence, but he would be blind not to notice how much he distracts me.

Like now, as he holds himself in his erect, businesslike posture, glaring at me with his perfect face. He's the kind of person who stays attractive even when angry, whose symmetry – as I've learned from weeks of googling what his designers mean by "ratio," – wouldn't break for the ugliest cry, the most serious deception. More simply put, as much as he turns me on, he's basically a robot. He's frightfully perfect.

In the typical Storm Woods fashion, every damn weekend has its own lesson plan. He has spent the past three months lecturing me about how to adjust to city life as a dragon shifter. But then, dragged me into the forest, before I have time to leave the office and even experience the city.

For some reason, however, he believes these diatribes transfer well to the forest:

"That was pathetic," he declares in frustration. "You need to channel your energy, not let it flow at random. If you continue like this in the city, you'll be found out within a month."

On today's "search for inspiration," we have finally set foot into "step two" territory, or breathing fire. Of course, this is to no avail. I feel the sparks in my throat like all dragon shifters do, and I inhale to kindle them, but somewhere between the inhalation and the exhale, or the blow, things fall apart. Fire simply goes everywhere, like some sort of ashy vomit.

No wonder Storm didn't want me around his place, or worse still, in his office. It would be reduced to ash in no time.

But I couldn't help thinking that this was not the only reason that he didn't want me around him there.

When we were in company, it was like I was invisible. If we were together in his office and someone came in, he almost instantly dismissed me without a second thought.

Other times, he would turn me into the butt of the office joke, which of course everyone else enthusiastically joined in with.

Don't get me wrong, I'm not some shrinking violet, completely unable to handle myself.

And I am, after all, the office junior there – the latest intern.

I guess it's the duty of the senior staff to make fun and send me on pointless errands – and so they do, with gusto.

It's just that Storm never displays this vibe with me when we're on our own together. Far from it.

He is tetchy, he is remote, he is creepy as fuck. He is either far too interested in me or peering down at me from afar, like some distant being on a cloud.

The one thing he is categorically not is jocular. Or fun of any description.

Until someone like Silverton sticks his nose around the door. Suddenly, then he either ignores me completely or starts joking around with him.

My clothing is the usual butt of most of Silverton's jibes.

"Dear God, what is he wearing today Storm? Never mind the fire-breathing – that suit is enough to short circuit the whole room..."

It was only day three of my internship. I still hadn't had the opportunity to go to a Storm Woods approved store and be reborn again, in the faithful image of my overlord.

Silverton paced up to me, once again in those suave heels that clicked together annoyingly with every footstep.

How I wanted to ask him about the cowboy boots that my father had mentioned. That would shut him up.

"I mean look at him, Storm, he's like some sort of less animated scarecrow. Where the heck did you get those pants kid? Rumpelstiltskin?"

With all the other staff around in Woods Interior Solutions, this is just something that is genuinely laughed off. With Silverton, there seems to be an air of menace behind it.

From the mystifying comments about my father to the way that he interacts with Storm, one thing is for sure. He is more than chief designer in this place.

Once or twice I have seen him put his hand on Storm's shoulder, in a way that suggests that they could be equals or even more than that.

This isn't something I have ever seen from any of the others. In fact, I am struggling to think of a single other person with whom Storm is so intimate with.

I guess I can't help but speculate on the nature of their relationship. Storm is no monk and I quickly gather that he is known around all the nightspots and clubs locally.

He has a lot of success with men, but usually, they are a good few years younger than Silverton. He is a lot older, by all accounts than his usual type.

Most of the guys he is reputed to go for are all around my age. This is something that sits oddly with me. But, from making some discreet inquiries, I discover that he seldom sees the same man more than a couple of times – a handful at best.

Despite being in vigorous mid-life, he has never shown any signs of slowing or even settling down, God forbid.

This can't help but leave me thinking that his interest – such as it is – in me is probably much the same. But, the only thing that I can't compute about that theory is why he has not already made a move.

The one thing that I have gleaned from my casual investigations around town is that Storm is a fast worker. Mighty fast.

It wouldn't usually take him days- let alone weeks- to work his way up to his prey, that's for sure.

This could mean one of two things, either he is not really interested in me and I have misread all the signs badly -not something I believe to be the case. Or that there is more to his attraction for me than the purely physical.

And that is a hard thing to swallow, too.

So exactly where Silverton and his phantom cowboy boots fit into the equation, I am not quite sure. All I know is that they seem close.

I know it has not been that long since I have been here, but Storm does not exactly strike me as the type of man to have a lot of close buddies.

He has acquaintances, business contacts, colleagues, and staff. He even has associates and contemporaries. One thing that he seems to have a distinct lack of is friends.

This immediately makes me think of my dad.

Despite their obvious differences, both in personality and well, just about everything apart from the whole dragon shifting thing – they are both quite self-contained types.

My father wears his solitary nature on his sleeve. Someone like Storm, less so.

He hides his true self from the others around him. This joking around only when there is company is a case in point.

I haven't been here long, but can I see that he is the type of person to change in a crowd and to adapt to what that person might be expecting of him.

And this kind of surprises me, I have got to say. Because from my first impressions of Storm Woods was that he was uncompromising and difficult.

Don't get me wrong, he still is. To me. And to the world at large, but it is just... strange.

Maybe I am not explaining this too clearly.

He is like a chameleon that changes to suit the people around him, but never in the ways that you are expecting. And not necessarily to please the people around him. But just to make the right kind of impression on them.

If he feels he needs to make his mark in a meeting or in a group of people, then he will do so. If he thinks they need to be charmed, he can turn that on at will. It is like clockwork. To me, he is like a robot, smooth with his patter and divorced from any spark of humanity. But, to them, he is on their wavelength.

It is certainly strange watching him operate, that's for sure.

Maybe it's because of his celebrity. He is used to performing or acting in a certain way in front of the media spotlight and attention that his work has brought him.

There always seems to be someone from some interior design magazine fawning about him, ready to include him in one of their color spreads.

But as flamboyant and stagy as the public persona of Storm Woods Inc is, the real man is even stranger.

It is hardly surprising that I don't yet know how to behave or act around him. I don't know what he wants me to do or how to get a grip of myself.

I don't exactly feel the most graceful before my trainer, and even less so when I consider how much I want to impress him. As much as we have butted heads in the past three months, I haven't put myself past considering the man my possible future lover.

Storm Woods clears his throat. He's on the verge of losing his patience.

"Before I shift myself and demonstrate for you again," he grumbles, "I want to see you try again. Focus on something this time; that will help you immensely."

I pray Storm Woods doesn't act on his words. Shifting involves removing one's clothes and, let me tell you, Storm Woods' shifting would distract me more than I already am.

It's not as if he hasn't already done so, like he has said, in an attempt to "demonstrate" to me what needs to be done.

Maybe it is hardly surprising that his little tutorials haven't had the desired effect. I could hardly stop myself from gawping at him.

But then he knew that was going to happen anyway.

The first time that he did so, it came as quite a surprise, let me tell you.

Compounded by the fact that, at that moment in time, I didn't know that the act of shifting means the removal of clothing.

I mean, when I shifted, on that fateful summer's night, I hadn't realized that my clothes had come off – until it was too late.

I guess it is either remove them yourself or discover your favorite sweater and pants in charred remains at your scaly feet.

Anyway, yes, the first time Storm had neglected to tell that small detail and so I had suddenly just turned around to see him standing there, butt naked in front of me.

"Right, so this is how we do it," he said, in a commanding tone of voice.

As you can imagine, this had my imagination racing.

I can tell that he enjoyed teasing me, especially that first time, in the woods.

There is no way I was encouraging a repeat performance of Storm removing his clothing or an action replay of my repressed responses to it.

I had better just focus on the task at hand and try to find the fire within, literally.

But it is so much harder than it feels like it ought to be.

When Storm demonstrates, it is like a seamless roll of flames, emanating gracefully from the center of his throat.

He just holds back his head, coughs a little and then this torrent of orange appears.

He can breathe small flames or absolute fireballs if he wants to.

Man, he can set fire to just about everything. I can now see why he brought half a dozen fire extinguishers with him, in that battle bus that he calls a camper van.

We have had to avert a forest fire a couple of times, although, to be fair, this has been usually down to my misplaced fiery utterances.

"Direct it! You've got to direct it right! We don't want the entire woodland to go up in smoke!"

Somehow, Storm seems to have mastered the ability to burn at will, but ensure that the object of his fiery fury has been sufficiently isolated to prevent the chance of inferno.

"Try something next to that lake so it doesn't burn too much. Go on. Over there. That tree branch"

Attempting to keep my superior at bay, I focus on a clump of leaves that hangs from a nearby tree. The dry mass has turned a fiery shade of orange in the approaching autumn. I will myself to become as angry or impassioned as the color suggests, vying for a strong emotion that will ignite a spark.

I sigh. Occasionally although I am either in danger of incinerating anything that comes into contact with me, my main problem is that I simply cannot raise a spark.

And my mind, evidently not out of adolescence, decides to focus on Storm's eyes.

It isn't long before this image gives way to arousal. I hesitate, turning to hide my erection from a man who would take one look at it, and laugh. I fear making an overt display of sexual attraction before someone so painfully aware of my ineptitude. He would only mock me for thinking I could have someone so much more experienced and qualified – in business and in shifting – than myself; I would only repeat my graduation disaster.

"You're already letting your mind get the better of you!" Storm shouts from a distance. "Is this really what your father has allowed you to become? Is this really the type of thing they do to dragons in Carlsbad?"

Again, with the dad stuff.

Yes, I think, this is what they do to dragons in Carlsbad.

Hell, even newcomers get a bad rap if they act in any way out of the ordinary. In what world could an outed dragon shifter walk free in a small town or anywhere, for that matter? It what version of Carlsbad – or any small town, for that matter – could any gay person do the same?

Like so many physical instruction teachers I have known, Storm remains helplessly wedded to the idea that success is all down to shouting.

Psychology or motivational thinking seems to play no part in his technique.

It is simply all YELL... YELL... YELL... with a nice sideline in ego chipping and sniping comments.

To make matters more stressful, Storm Woods is as relentless about fire-breathing as he was, about shifting.

"River, River," he chides from across the way. "You really need to stop letting those silly morals and preconceptions of yours get in the way. Do you think I became as successful as I am by squashing my passionate side? Do you think I hold back, avoid trying new things, just because I'm afraid?"

I turn, and he raises an eyebrow. The glimmer in his amber eyes tells me that he senses my sexually-charged response, which he, himself has ignited. I haven't been able to hide from him before, and this moment gives proof that my emotions are no exception.

I feel myself glower self-consciously, which only makes everything worse.

Storm rolls his eyes dramatically at my blush and feels myself blush even more deeply.

This is so fucking unfair.

Does he like seeing me so embarrassed? Because it is starting to feel as if he is getting me into these heightened states for nothing more than his own gratification.

Does he want me to fuck him or is he just into humiliation?

I try again, closing my eyes and drawing on my deepest reserves of energy.

It is not that I am even attempting to hide it, at this point. I just want him to do something about it. He is the teacher in this scenario, after all.

He knows nothing I do not, and he knows how magnetic I find him, I have nothing to lose.

I face the clump of leaves again, this time allowing my mind to wander. I picture Storm and me in his office; I sprawled in the leather chair that sits across from his towering throne.

I know he was looking at me that day, that first time when I was in his office. And always has done ever since.

Who cares whatever that creep Silverton came out with.

He doesn't think I am second place to anyone. And certainly not to him.

If there a Storm and him at all?

Yes, occasionally, I might get a faint whiff of something between the two of them, but it doesn't feel as strong as the pull that he is showing towards me right now.

And as for whatever he was going on about, I decide in my mind to pay it no more attention.

I write him off as a jealous older man who, whilst we're at it, hasn't aged all that well.

I don't see him as having any sort of power over Storm.

In fact, I am not even too sure why I am thinking so much about Silverton Wolf or whatever his name is.

He is getting in the way.

Finally putting Silverton Wolf out of my mind, I can get down to business.

Now I am getting somewhere.

I can see Storm in front of me. I am curled into his oversized leather chair, spinning around.

It has captivated his attention. I have captivated his attention. I can see it now. He wants me to make him beg...

I imagine him crouched on his knees before me, teaching me how to control a spark, not unlike the one that builds from my stomach to my throat, and how to release it steady, steady, and just for him.

I feel a twitching in my lower abdomen, and I inhale. Air puffs into my chest and my stomach, swirling the powerful energy toward its only exit.

I begin to exhale, supporting my stomach to bring a smooth, consistent stream of fire out of my esophagus. The heat burns dry on my face, searing my eyes shut.

Then, memories of the past cut into focus. I witness once again my classmates fleeing from view, old friends avoiding me for fear I may endanger them. I feel the pain that followed that horrid night, the pain of loneliness, anguish, and guilt. A sob lurches forth to cut off the flame.

"Think about your target!" I hear Storm shout faintly behind me, probably reading my thoughts, again.

I fix my gaze on the leaves. I want to think about the present. I want to think about what gives me passion now.

That party didn't happen, I tell myself. I kissed that boy, that nameless boy, and we both had a fantastic night.

No one in Carlsbad cares that I'm gay. They're only mad because I turned out better than them, that I have the potential to become more than they are.

I left home and went to school and have good grades. Most of them didn't do that, and now it's something they regret. They regard me with envy and with fear.

I fabricate a new affirmation with every strong breath. It hurts to lie to myself this way, but it does not hurt as badly as the fire that singes my lips.

Am I doing this right?

It seems a lot hotter and a lot more intense than the one or two little sparks that I have managed to produce in the past.

Even when I nearly set the camper van on fire, it was more of a fluke than anything else – one of my sparks connecting near the gas tank and sending Storm into the biggest panic I have ever seen him in.

The image of him like that, running around and yelling and waving his arms around simultaneously makes me giggle, but also want to dominate him.

This is the thought in my mind that I need in order to raise a flame that is capable of striking my target.

My vision tunnels. I catch a glimpse of the flaming branch before everything goes black.

Chapter 18

Storm

The burning branch falls to the ground, extinguished by the cool mud that springs free from the earth. It is a shame that we dragon shifters must lay waste to nature, something so eternally inspiring, to perfect our art. Perhaps this is why we have winter, so we can prey on withering plants, or plants already dead.

But perfection does not always come with skill, as demonstrated by the perfect boy who lays unconscious at my feet, covered in his own ejaculation.

As disgusting as it sounds, and as without grace, as the situation seems, the result is just as I assumed. River would have found success so much sooner if he had embraced his passion – that is, his attraction to me – instead of letting his fears get in the way.

If only he would so surrender, in his human form.

The desperate hope erupts forth before I can lay it to rest. I have no doubt, now, that the boy wants me. Yet, I still face the dilemma of how I will bring him to admit it.

The first step, I think humorously, is waiting for him to wake up.

I collect the boy's clothes, which he left several yards back, at our campsite. I fold his modest outfit and, as he lacks a pillow, prop the ensemble under his head. I remind myself to tell him, too, that he needs better weekend wear.

Covering him with his sleeping bag, I turn back to our woodland space. I clear our camping supplies – which include two tents, by the way – for the journey back to Chicago. Tucking the items into the van, I think how inconvenient it is that River hasn't yet mastered flight. We could travel far more efficiently without roads limiting our path, especially on a cloudy day, such as this one, where we could hide in plain view. In truth, flying is the most direct option.

I assure myself that we will move on to flying soon enough, after spending a few more weeks on fire-breathing. As excruciating as the process appears, I believe it's critical that River, as my pupil, learn as much as he can before his father forces him home to finish his final year of school.

I can't imagine somehow that Ashton is going to allow him to spend that much time here with me, despite what he said as a bargaining chip to get me to take him.

He is going to want him back at his college and then home again to Marsh Home and Hearth. This is going to be his literal only time to learn these skills. He doesn't have anyone else. I am his only hope.

But this is not all.

I cannot kid myself that the only thing that I have an interest in is his professional development as either a manager or a dragon.

So sure, I need him to get to grips with the basics of shifting.

But, I add to myself, the time it takes for him to master these skills will also give me more time to get him into my bed. He's already attracted to me, so why hasn't he made a move?

He's had twenty years to learn about how wrong he is, I argue with myself. He's only been punished for that sort of thing.

I shut the trunk with a slam, securing everything inside except myself and River. He lies, still comatose, several yards from me, and I refuse to wake him.

Shifting is exhausting, and he needs all the energy he can get to endure a normal workday, tomorrow.

I cannot let my advisors think that these excursions serve any purpose other than to collect inspiration for our new line of "earth-inspired" décor.

Locating a wide-trunked tree I seek some rest, recharging myself in case River, upon waking, comes to his senses.

Chapter 19

Storm

"Um, Storm?" Something pokes my shoulder, jolting me awake. I leap from the ground, startled that I allowed myself to fall completely out of consciousness.

River's tired eyes meet mine and, accentuated by dark circles and the aqua-colored evening, they glow bluer than before. I wish these crystal orbs were half as intense in dragon form, for they, I half-believe, would help me establish a connection with him. I entertain that, scientifically, we could reinforce our relationship just by looking at each other, but it would be a stretch.

Nonetheless, the boy's eyes, if as blue in dragon form, would make his powers appear more intense. I cannot underestimate the power of hue.

River quickly looks to the ground, denying me his gaze.

"Thank you," he brushes his dirt-stained jeans, "for bringing my clothes back to me."

He blushes fiercely. He knows I saw the aftermath, that I laid eyes upon his flaccid, post-orgasmic member. Although faintly, I sense he also detects that I, his professional acquaintance, know my role in arousing him.

"You're welcome," I say quietly, smirking into the shadows. "It's the least I could do, for someone who has finally grasped fire-breathing basics."

Unsurprisingly, the comment angers him, but he only utters the simple question, "The basics?"

"Of course," I reply, feeding into the banter. "Most dragon shifters are doing what you just did, as soon as they exit the womb. Although I admit, you're a special case."

I mention what I know will incite anger, for I want to see how far I can push him. I want to test his limits. I want to know what level of fury a shift requires.

He crosses his arms.

"My father didn't have time to teach me, you know. His business isn't big, but he doesn't have assistants who can take things over while we go 'camping.'"

He punctuates the word with his fingers, raising his voice sarcastically.

I cannot deny him. His father, against my desires, took over his family business and left his son alone with two difficult identities, one rejected by a handful of people and the second, by the world. I could not stop the family-minded Ashton Marsh. How could I have halted someone with a direct path to success?

Still, River's anger has driven him to express himself more than he has, in three months. This increased self-expression, this assertion of his true self, will help him immensely in combat. Dragons, while characterized by their ability to shift between human and creature, need a solid sense of self – a personality that remains concrete – through the physical changes. It is only after developing this identity that they can find power when action becomes necessary.

It will also help him in the bedroom. There, the need for confidence is more evident.

Chapter 20

River

My steps resemble stomps as I walk, angrily, to Storm Woods' van. It's a creepy-ass van, a perfect match for his creepy-ass self. To top things off, he uses the van exclusively for our weekend excursions. The only thing weirder is how much money he pays to rent a spot in his Chicago garage, to park it with his other, flashier, but nonetheless more normal, car.

I have wanted many times for him to stop training me in shifting. I long to tell him that being a dragon isn't why I'm in Chicago, damn it; understanding that he and my father have some secret pact, I would prefer he teach me some business tactics.

Another thing which, by the way, has not come to fruition. The man sits with his clients most of the day or spends hours chatting with them on the phone. He prattles on about "taste" and "style" with other eccentric, high-end personalities, leaving my training to his assistants rather than to himself.

What makes the situation even more frustrating is the fact that we can't even have productive alone time – that is, hours of uninterrupted sex fueled by our mutual passion and a fierce hatred for each other – during these weekends.

First, there is the sleeping situation. There are two tents in that weird looking camper van. If I had thought we were going to sleep in the van, then nope.

I'm not actually quite sure what the point of the damned stupid thing is, apart from having me nearly turn it into a fireball and the first item on the News at Six.

So, the pair of us turn in for the night, like boy scouts or something, once we are done toasting half of the forest with our flame projectiles.

It is like he is deliberately teasing me with his presence, right next to mine, but covered with thin canvas.

I have already discovered that he sleeps in the nude. That much has been apparent through the shadows in the tent at night.

I sit and wonder, during these long fall evenings, just what is the point of me being here and exactly what it was my father thought that Storm could teach me.

Despite being here for some time now, I have still not managed to fathom the exact nature of their relationship – nor that of Storm's myriad of other complex liaisons.

He gets me out here, into the fresh air and the open. We excite our passions and he has seen me in all sorts of embarrassing predicaments.

We get naked, for God's sake, and for what? To turn into dragons, one of which can barely breathe fire and can't fly worth shit. What joy, how fun. If I'm going to spend this much one-on-one time with Storm Woods, I might as well spend it indulging in the one thing I like about the man.

His genitalia, too, forms only one of his impressive physical characteristics. He keeps his body, underneath the business attire, as chiseled as his perfect face. The man looks like a statue, even when he, with red skin and bulging veins, shifts into his dragon form.

Once again, I wonder why we are sleeping in tents, on an uncomfortable ground mat and in flimsy individual sleeping bags, when there is a (relatively) cozy double bed in the camper van.

The camper van is something that no matter how hard I try, I can't quite get to grips with as being any part of Storm.

For a start off, the interior is glaringly hideous. It seems to have fallen straight out of the seventies, even though I theoretically know that the van is not quite that old.

Everything inside it seems to come in all five hundred unholy shades of brown.

But all the same, it is clean and serviceable and it looks as if the double bed, which pulls out from the side of the van, has barely been used.

Is being forced to sleep in discomfort, nursing one's lonely erection part and parcel of dragon school, I wonder?

Storm does not strike me as someone who is into denial in any way shape or form. What is the purpose of this torment?

Storm Woods climbs into the driver's side of the van, slamming the door behind him. He isn't someone to slam things, but the rusty van requires such force.

I momentarily worry that the whole thing will just fall apart.

It shudders and sways, but the sides just about hold it together.

He puts the key in the ignition, and the engine roars to life.

"I know I'm an asshole, but you're the oldest student I've had, especially as a child of a shifter. You haven't had constant experience from childhood; it is a complicated situation, indeed."

I wish he would stop reminding me that my father neglected me – or whatever it could be called when dragons don't teach their children to shift. I wish he would stop making perceptive comments out of the blue. I wish he would think about what he probably had to undergo to land his position because most self-made businesspeople begin kissing ass and changing themselves to please others.

Of course, shifting involves a different sort of change.

Storm Woods pulls us out of the forest in silence. His mouth, pressed into a flat line, nonetheless evidences how my comments have affected him, how my fury has surprised him. In fact, neither he nor I feel accustomed to the energy I have released.

But, when he again opens his mouth he addresses me calmly:

"You need to master fire breathing, a task best done after facing another fear – your sexuality. It saddens me to see that, even in this age, people shame you for who you're attracted to. With shifting, it really is a catch-22."

He sighs. His expression changes only minutely, and I find his glibness exasperating. Yeah, it's a catch-22, I want to say, and a little bit more than that. When you're not a rich and powerful interior designer who lives in one of the most diverse places in the country, I want to sneer, it makes life hell.

Storm Woods sighs, again, indicating that he, again, wants me to tell him something. But something more powerful than instinct tells me I can't spill my guts in front of a guy who already seems to know everything, and who might see my spilling as a weakness he can take advantage of.

However, Storm Woods doesn't continue with his voodoo magic mind reading. Instead, he simply admits:

"I left Carlsbad for almost the same reason, you know."

"Really?" my eyes become saucers, and I gasp. There's no way this man left from that small town due to shame alone, not with his worldly knowledge and, frankly, his haughty attitude.

"Yes. Don't get me wrong, I was different in many other ways, but who I love was what booted me from the region. Even my dad, who had raised me alone – much like your father – didn't want me around. Thankfully, that rejection gave me the motivation to become bigger, and better than all of them."

I roll my eyes at the amount of egotistical self-centeredness Storm Woods managed to cram into such a short tale but, faults aside, the story pulls at my heartstrings.

But Storm Woods isn't finished.

"I'm surprised your father didn't tell you, seeing as how he knows you're gay. I thought he would have given you more information since he sent you here alone."

I shake my head in the negative.

"He told me I have a lot in common with you, that's it. He also said you had worked together on some stuff, which makes sense because, you know," my tongue ties, "fireplaces go in houses."

Perhaps I sell our relationship short by considering these things minor, but I reason that our past and our dragon shifter status are, even now, the only things we have in common.

"Perhaps," Storm Woods replies pensively, "he wants our relationship to remain professional. Or perhaps – excuse my vulgarity – he wanted to avoid my teaching you other sorts of, um, non-business-related materials."

I understand, now, his reference to sex. The man takes his eyes completely off the road, staring me straight in the face. His eyes glow brighter and more orange than I have ever observed.

Chapter 21

I do a pitiful job hiding my smirk. I pray the boy will occupy himself with his phone or the side-view window, even on the relatively empty highway.

The mile markers zip past, showing me there are only a few more miles to go. I swallow hard, stifling the heat in my lower abdomen that threatens, oh-so-intensely, to overwhelm my lower extremities. I need my feet to drive, damn it: my legs can't turn to jelly yet.

Or ever, really, if he chokes like I assume he will. He wants to dominate me, he thinks, but he hasn't reached that level of confidence. He won't tell me his desire to become my superior; he still believes that such a statement will injure my ego.

Minutes later, and we edge within yards of privacy, of freedom. I park the van in the garage which, on a Sunday evening, has hardly an empty spot. Chicago, so modern, still takes Sunday as a day of rest. Even in a time, a place where things appear to have progressed, we retain some of that old-world conservatism.

Not quite as bad as Carlsbad, granted. That place is on lockdown on a Sunday.

River had told me that Ashton had tried to open the kingdom of Marsh Hearth and Home on a Sunday, a few years ago.

The locals organized a petition against it and forced them to close.

This tale of parochialism made me smirk until I realized that in some ways the denizens of Chicago weren't that much better - despite their well-polished exterior.

One thousand and one coffee emporiums and a smattering of nose rings does not preclude city dwellers from being as prissy about some traditional things, as much as the rural hillbillies they love to mock.

Their sensibilities can be even more censorious than the rednecks, especially when it comes to their sense of liberal outrage.

But politics aside, there is still an element of the conservative, even here.

Why else have I been hiding River away in the forest for us to continue his studies?

Well, I suppose it's fleeting conservatism, anyway. I order the boy to follow me. His white face and glazed eyes tell me he couldn't have conceived otherwise, that he might have wandered into my place without my beckoning.

This is the first time he has been around here. The first time that he has set foot in my apartment. I can see the wonder and surprise in his face, as he pokes his head around and finally sees the interior design of my bedroom at last.

My professional pride has to be beaten down in order to prevent myself from launching a probe of his considered opinion of the décor. I am still trying to get the boy to see things from a design perspective, but unfortunately, from the bland suit he wore to our first encounter, to the mediocre slacks he has presented himself in since, I despair at ever winning him over.

Slacks or no, River enters my apartment a bit like a lamb to the slaughter.

He looks at me with those perfect cyan eyes and still, even after three months in the city, he looks as pure as ever.

This is not what I have been hoping for although, of course, he is irresistible to me.

He simply stands there in front of me, with that look, as if I am his master and he is the disciple.

Or possibly the slave.

So submissive already, the boy. I don't bother to lock the door once we enter my domain.

I hold him to the wall, the light pressure of my hand mastering his body, and ask him what he wants.

His answer elicits no surprise, on my end. He says he wants me to fuck him, pure and simple. However, his eyes, glowing that brilliant blue under the streetlamp glow that shines through my undrawn drapes, squint in regret. He wants to dominate me, I can see it, but I can only intrude so far into his thoughts.

We make love – and yes, I say love because I feel it – violently and passionately. I guide him. I give him the methods of domination, just as I gave them in the forest. To our final throes, I leave it to him to listen.

Chapter 22

River

We enter the city limits within an hour. Storm Woods' final statement has left my head spinning for most of the journey. I know, within a reasonable doubt, his attraction to me.

But he wants to teach me what, exactly? I can only guess according to the smirk he has held since revealing his sexuality. I suspect that I won't call home about whatever the lesson becomes.

Storm Woods parks his massive van under his antique apartment complex, then beckons me to follow him.

"No, dear, you're not going home, not yet."

His language, melodic and flirtatious, and his walk, fluid and relaxed, tell me he's already in the mood.

About time. I can't help thinking. But I don't say anything.

It has taken three months to get to this point. The last thing I want to do is say anything that might put Storm off his stride.

I think it is fair to say that we get on better when we don't speak.

I mean, if the guy just shut up a bit more. I might get on with him a bit better.

When we speak, we come at cross purposes to each other. In other words, the guy gets on my tits.

After an awkward elevator ride, Storm throws open the door to his living space.

The interior looks surprisingly new for a building constructed in the early-1900s, but, needless to say, Storm's personality makes up for the lack of old-Chicago charm. He has decorated the spacious studio just as I imagined: with neutral colored furniture, ornate decorations, and colorful artwork hanging from the walls.

I can't fault the décor in the apartment, but it somehow strikes me as exactly what I would have expected, which in some strange sort of way is not quite what I expected.

I suppose I thought he would have surprised me more.

Still, like him, the apartment is a modern masterpiece. Exquisite, tasteful, hard to pin down but possibly just a mirage and not representative of what lurks beneath.

"I think it's time we cut the bullshit." Storm Woods tosses his keys on his island kitchen counter, "You want to fuck me, or, more accurately, you want me to fuck you."

In all honesty, I had wanted the opposite, but I nodded nonetheless.

Maybe I am not ready yet to approach him as an equal. Maybe, he is not ready yet for me to do so. Whichever it is, I am not going to argue.

Storm Woods presses himself against me, whispering in my ear,

"Come on, I want more than that. Tell me what you want." He presses his lips to my neck and releases his hot breath onto the thin flesh. I shiver.

"Tell me," Storm Woods demands.

"I, I, ah..." I moan before I can verbalize my arousal so strong, I must do something to relieve it.

Storm Woods' mind reading abilities come to the rescue. He cups between my legs, massaging, making standing difficult, even against a wall. My erection pressed against my jeans, painfully hard.

Storm Woods guides me to his sofa, pressing small kisses on my face. As soon as I sit he unbuttons my jeans, allowing my arousal to spring free.

"Do what you need to do," he guides my hand to my member, "to tell me what you want. Guide your passion, my love."

My love. God.

I run my hand over my sensitive skin, breathing deeper and heavier with each stroke;

"I want," I stammer, "I want you to fuck me."

In this moment, I make an honest avowal. How could I have dominated Storm Woods, like I had in my dreams?

Storm Woods kisses me on the mouth.

"Good," he purrs, working my underwear down my knees.

He kisses the inside of my thighs, making small grunts between each kiss. My erection grows harder and I moan again, wishing he would do something to release the tension.

"No," he stops abruptly. "Be direct. Tell me what you want."

I can't believe he can speak so clearly, even in heated passion. I would give to express myself half as well under normal conditions, another strike against my dominatrix dreams.

I struggle to align my thoughts, to make the words come out.

"I want you to fuck me."

For some reason, I think putting emphasis on a prior statement will satisfy him.

And it doesn't.

"I know," he looks up at me, raising an eyebrow. "Perhaps I can guide you. How do you want me to fuck you?"

In any way that makes you stop the pedagogical bullshit and get in my ass, is what I think, but I only utter the final three words.

"That's...adequate," he mutters, standing. From where I sit, I see clearly that Storm Woods is just as aroused as I am. He waves his hand in his typical manner, moving to a partitioned section at the back of his apartment.

"Follow me."

Chapter 23

River

Storm Woods, far from what you would call a large man, has a massive bed. It's orange sheets, I notice, hypersensitive from months among Chicago's fashionable elite, will not clean up well. What drove him, I wonder, to choose an ensemble so delicate?

But Storm Woods, pushing me onto the cushions, doesn't seem to care. His member has grown more erect since the living room, I notice, for he neglects to fall into the sheets alongside me.

Indeed, in an outstanding display of stamina, Storm Woods unfastens his jeans and pulls them, along with his underwear, to his knees.

"I want you," he caresses the back of my head with his hand, "to suck me."

He draws my head toward his naked cock before I can protest. My own arousal aches so strongly, I cannot possibly hold out for him. Unable to resist, however, I wrap my lips around his member, running my tongue along his shaft.

Yet my hands have other plans. I fondle myself, but Storm Woods calls me to stop.

"Resist the urge," he commands from above. "Control it, and you will come out stronger. It will feel so good, oh…" he trails off.

Sexual pleasure, as it turns out, can bring even the most powerful, intimidating people to their knees.

However, I myself can only last so long. After a few more minutes of oral stimulation, I feel myself about to burst.

"I can tell you're growing restless,"

Storm Woods affirms what I feel, from up top. He pulls my head away and stares straight into my eyes.

"On your back," he directs.

I submit, prostrating on command upon the heavily-cushioned mattress. Compared to my own bed, it feels like I'm floating on clouds. Storm Woods balances himself on top of me, pressing his fingers into my backside in preparation for entry. I whimper under his touch, unsure, in my current condition, if we will ever reach true penetration.

Storm Woods kisses me again and hushes me.

"I promise," he whispers, "it'll feel so much better if you hold it in. Breathe. Don't come until you can't hold it anymore, beautiful. Control."

Beautiful. My hips jolt forward, but Storm Woods presses them into the mattress while repeating his mantra, "control."

Slowly he presses himself into me. We proceed in a rocking motion, timed by the sound of our bodies coming together. I breathe into my stomach, unable to suppress the moans that escape the back of my throat and, by his own heated grunts, I detect Storm Woods has found the same difficulty. A few moments more and he falters, filling me with his own hot energy. I feel the same just seconds later, melting in my own release.

My energy falls away and, in a moment, everything goes black.

Chapter 24

Storm

Watching River sleep is even more adorable when he's in my bed. I tuck the sheets around him, showering myself before climbing in by his side. The silent night envelopes the two of us, and I, mysteriously less sleepy than my companion, use this time to ruminate.

Did he notice, I wonder, what I told him as we made love? Of course, he must have inferred, for I told him nothing.

At least here, he took my advice. I find his directness invigorating, and his ability to channel energy, especially during sex, gives me hope for the future.

He has the feeling yet, like a good son, he keeps it chained. Not all is lost, but our relationship would have become far more eventful far more quickly, had he launched himself fully into his passions.

Then, a sort-of fear worms its way into my consciousness. In the heat of the moment, we neglected to use protection. As an un-diseased individual, I would not hold this oversight in any critical regard but, in the dragon world, failure to protect oneself can prove deadly.

My heart races but, somewhat ironically, holding my lover, I manage some sleep.

Chapter 25

River

It is a few days later. Fall is turning colder and wetter.

It is not that I am exactly having pangs of regret for leaving Carlsbad. But it is strange not to see the changing seasons quite so upfront as I am used to.

Of course, there are trees in Chicago. There are even saplings planted in containers inside the premises of Woods Interior Solutions, although, these are evergreen trees and not deciduous.

It has never occurred to me before that I am a country boy. But in the gray soupy cloud of the city fall weather, I do kind of miss some other acknowledgment of the season we are in than just the relentless rain.

Carlsbad now would be a delicious mixture of golden hues and soulful landscapes. I guess I never even noticed the beauty of the backdrop to the town – I was just so desperate to leave its' foreground.

It's funny, for someone who has never felt the need to go outdoors particularly, but living in a city now feels weird. Yeah, they still have weather and season changes. There is still a breeze that comes in off the lake that we can feel.

Feel, but can't see from the offices I work in or the apartment that I sleep in.

Sometimes, I find myself feeling a little dispirited at the concrete and tarmac that covers everything. I never noticed that I liked having nature so close at hand.

Then I smile at myself, suddenly, for having turned into Mother Nature's son since arriving in Chicago.

If Storm misses rural life, it doesn't show. He is more than up for the nights out on the town, the endless party lifestyle that his affluent life affords and the shallow pleasures of the bars and clubs that accompany it.

So far though, he has never taken me out to any of them.

It is not as if it bothers me particularly. It just confuses me.

Storm is hardly a repressed person. As he keeps lecturing me, there is no need to be clandestine here in Chicago. Theoretically, nobody cares about his sexuality. Or mine.

So why does he only ever see me in private?

I am not sure what the deal is. But all our dealings, if you can call them that, seem to be accomplished either in the dead of some forsaken woodlands – or in his apartment, strictly after hours and when there is no one else around.

In the office, he still either blanks me totally or joins in mocking my rural ways to the rest of the staff.

This doesn't matter, I have got used to it.

And maybe, I tell myself, I am not really up for anything resembling a relationship with the guy.

Perhaps, this sex only agreement would work just fine for me. But I don't quite get the impression that this is actually what Storm wants.

For someone who spends most of his time berating me for not being passionate enough, I can't help feeling that he is hiding a part of him away. Even now, even after some months have passed.

It surprised me that it had taken so long to even get to this point. And Storm does not strike me as being someone who is slow to get what he wants.

Despite all his talk of unleashing what is within, he is still resisting. Still hiding something from me. It's like he wants something from me, but won't quite tell me what it is.

And that is really not like Storm at all.

If all he wanted from me was sex, then surely, he wouldn't be taking all this trouble to teach me how to achieve the perfect fucking shift.

It's not even that I really care anymore about it. I am only going along with it to please Storm.

It perplexes me that after all this time, I still want his approval.

That confuses me because as a person, Storm Woods really fucking annoys me sometimes.

And yet, there I still am. Every weekend or every second weekend – depending on Storm's hectic work and social life schedule – we are back in those goddam woodlands.

Now in a way it is quite nice to see some nature again after a whole week of tarmac or asphalt – like I was saying. It makes a good change to the whole jaded city living thing.

But, Jesus, it is beginning to get cold now and still, Storm insists on us sleeping in those two separate – and quite flimsy tents.

It makes me wonder what he has brought his horror show of a camper van for.

Despite the plummeting temperatures, Storm still sleeps in the nude and I still regularly have to dispense with clothing as the fall turns into winter.

I can't help wondering when our dragon studies will be concluded for the year. Yet somehow, Storm seems impervious to temperature.

One thing that he is not completely immune to is the attitude of others.

Well, one person in particular.

It would seem that Storm's absence on the nightclub circuit or whatever the hell it is that gay dragons get up to in cities, has been noted.

By Silverton.

I would be there, innocently minding my own business in the office, whilst he would be parading about, atop of those ridiculous clickety clackety heels that he insisted on wearing. And all the while having the nerve to turn to me and giving me this goddam superior look.

Substitute cowboy boots.

I hide a smirk as I envisaged him in the full get up; Stetson hat, rhinestone, and a ridiculous buckle belt.

Idly, I find myself wondering if he had also been taken aside by Storm and remodeled from the toe to the top like I had.

That had been an interesting afternoon. Storm had dragged me out of the office one day and more or less propelled me into one of the trendiest men's shops in Chicago.

To say that I felt out of place there would have been an understatement. He got me kitted out by a smiling shop assistant with blue hair and an ironic tattoo, who couldn't seem to help himself from sneering at my department store suit and sensible haircut.

I guess I have never been much of a follower of fashion, or very interested in clothes. But all this would have to change if I was going to remain working in Woods Interior Solutions.

"He's clashing with the interiors. Sort him out will you"" said Storm, throwing down a fistful of money on the counter.

The blue haired youth sniggered, as he ushered me towards the changing rooms with his tape measure and so began one of the most uncomfortable two and a half hours of my life.

Every single bit of my anatomy was sized up, literally and figuratively by Travis the tape measure-wielding sadist.

Then I was presented with an ominous parade of ripped T-shirts, skinny pants, and other horrific "casual" wear.

"That's just for starters. I still expect something a little more fitting for the office" snapped Storm to Travis. He shot him a commanding look, his amber orange flecked eyes glaring with disdain.

It seemed like he and Travis knew each other well.

Another of his conquests, no doubt, I thought, as my eyes rolled upwards in the perfectly sterile cubicle.

We didn't get out of there until Storm had spent upwards of $1000 and I had every manner of suit – ranging from the most casual to the most formal.

"Look at that," said Storm, finally satisfied as I emerged from the changing room for the ten thousandth time.

"Not one single strand of polyester. At last."

"So, I um am to wear this in the office then," I asked as I trotted out after Storm, carrying all the paper bags to his car.

"Yes River, you are to wear them to the office." He turned to me briskly "But keep this won't you?"

Storm held up my old suit, delicately, between his fingertips, wrinkling up his nose in disgust like he had just pulled a dead rat out of a sewer.

"You want me to keep it?"

"Yeah. We can use it as target practice the next time you're breathing fire"

The first time my suit made its' debut in the office, it elicited a spontaneous round of applause from the staff.

The first chance Silverton got to corner me, as soon as the room cleared, he was there.

Fuck me, he was one ugly dude, I thought, as his lank gray hair fell over his face and into the accounts sheet I was working on.

"Storm's looking for his ideas book," said Silverton briskly, pushing me aside. "It's in that drawer"

"Well, excuse me" I muttered.

Silverton pulled the notebook out on top of the desk. Inside it, something else fell on to the table where I was working.

A hard-backed journal or book that looked rather dog-eared.

I picked it up idly.

Silverton's shifty gray colored eyes flashed at me oddly. He seemed to be inviting me to have a look at it, as he gathered the notepad he had come in for.

"You don't want this?" I said, waving the second booklet at him.

As I did so, a loose sheet fluttered out of the pad.

It was in Storm's handwriting.

Assuming it was just another design notebook, I picked it up and began reading it.

"No" he smirked, watching me. "But maybe you should, you might learn something"

Then, something strange happened. Suddenly Silverton's unpleasant features were right up close and besides my face, watchfully.

"Like I said. You're playing second fiddle. You're a poor substitute for your father"

And with that, he flounced off on those ridiculous heels.

Chapter 26

Storm

'June 12th; So, he has done what he said he was going to do and he has taken him back, away from me.

He told me as much before. With that self-satisfied look upon his face. He said he would get Ashton away from me and so he did.

This morning, as I was preparing to leave Carlsbad and go back to the university, he suddenly turns around and announces that he is getting married.

Married.

Fucking married.

Just like that.

"What did you just say," I asked, trying to keep my voice light and airy, but all the while, the blood was just going whoosh around my head.

"Yeah. Isn't it great?" he said, with a gigantic smile stretching out across his face.

And he looked so gorgeous. So genuinely happy, that it hurt my heart and seemed to make it fluctuate in its beating.

"Married, as in, to a woman" I heard my voice say.

"Of course, to a woman" scoffed Ashton.

His muscular frame towering over me. He pushed his brown colored hair out of his eyes in that casual way of his, that drove me mad. He must know that it drives me mad surely?

Is it really possible for another human being to be so totally and completely fucking oblivious to another's feelings, I wonder to myself?

Yes, it is, especially when that person comes from Carlsbad.

"Well, that's news to me," I say faintly.

This was the first I had heard of any woman let alone a fiancée.

Clearly, this is the work of Beelzebub Marsh Aka daddy Silus.

Just like he said he would, he was managing to split us up.

I mean, the metaphorical us that existed in my mind, at least.

I had to admit that the actual physical us did not quite extend to that.

Just that one, fleeting moment, in Arbuckle's Lake, when he turned towards me and sent me that look and in the heat of that summer's night I finally leaned forward to kiss his perfect face....'

Chapter 27

I slam the journal shut abruptly.

My heart is suddenly in my mouth, pounding crazily.

Oh, My God.

I had no idea. No idea at all that this was even a thing.

I sit and stare at the perfectly chosen shade of beige wall in front of me.

So that is what the sly old weasel meant. That is why he has been taunting me all this time.

Although I suppose I had suspected that someone as louche as Storm had feelings for my father back then – it was still a shock to see them written down in black and white like that.

My heart is still pounding hard. I am not quite sure what to think.

I suppose that that creep Silverton thinks that I should be jealous.

But then, I am guessing that is because how he feels about me.

Instead of being angry or upset at Storm – or my dad – I find a smile curling around my lips.

This has proved two things;

That that sad old creep Silverton feels threatened by mine and Storm's relationship – such as it is.

And that Storm was actually a human being once.

More than that, it has offered a rare glimpse into the strange world of both he and my father being teenagers.

Imagining one's own father as teenager – never mind one with complicated feelings – let alone potentially gay ones, in that day and age – well, this is never something that I have fully appreciated before.

It is quite a lot to take on board.

From reading that extract, it seems as if Storm did indeed have some sort of crush on my dad.

And, just from the very short amount that I had read, it seemed as if it was an unrequited one.

Now that is a topic that is close to my heart. I probably could have chosen my major in unrequited crushes, so I know how it feels.

Imagining my buttoned-up father with the incredibly controlling teenage Storm is a bizarre thought.

Even more intriguing is the thought that Storm did not get his own way for once.

Or at least, that is what I assume happened.

I haven't read the rest of it...

But should I?

In fact, should I really have even read this portion of it?

This is someone's confidential diary – even if it is from more than two decades before.

I shouldn't really be reading it all.

Not only is it morally dubious, but I might get caught doing so.

I sit there for a few minutes, drumming my fingers on the desk.

This is hard. So hard.

I am trying like crap to do the right thing, when I swear to God a fierce fall wind whistles through the window and lifts the book open, again.

The pages ripple with the breeze running through it and eventually fall open in the middle of the journal.

On to a page marked;

"July 2nd"

Despite myself and my best intentions, I find myself leaning over it and pouring over the spidery writing that continues...

Chapter 28

Ashton

The day he first shifted was the same day he came out to me.

We were at the lake. It was the one at the end of my grandfather's old land.

Because it was technically on private property, it tended to be deserted most of the time. Even on achingly hot summer days like this.

Although the land surrounding my grandfather's old house no longer belonged to our family, the guy who owned it now didn't mind too much if we came back to it from time to time.

Sometimes my dad would come up here to fish, but today, Storm and I were just hanging out.

It was too hot to do anything other than just strip off and sit there, sinking our feet into the ice-cold water beneath us and sip some of the now-far-too-warm soda that he had brought in his flask.

"I wish we had some beer," I said.

This was about the first thing that either of us had said for more than half an hour. It was far too hot to speak.

School was over forever and we were in the long, slow month of August, filled with what seemed like eternal sunshine.

In a few weeks' time, Storm was off to college and I would be left here, on my own, in a small town that hated anyone a bit different.

How he had tried his hardest to get me to take an interest and apply to the college as well. But I hadn't.

I just couldn't say that it held any interest for me.

As bad as Carlsbad was at times, there were still things here for me. The nature. The countryside. The places to find to escape to.

Maybe I wasn't the most conscientious shifter in the history of dragons, but if you wanted to find the right setting to shift into a mythical being, then Carlsbad was the place to do it.

All in all, the bright lights and proximity to nosy strangers that Chicago threatened, was just an unwelcome intrusion for me.

Plus, the fact that I was tremendously unacademic and didn't fancy spending the next three or four years watching all the jerks from school pouring beer down their necks and pursuing their jackass buddies.

I'd rather just stay put, thanks.

But this was a point of view that Storm couldn't see, couldn't follow and couldn't understand.

We had rowed about it and for the last twenty-five minutes, he had been sitting there, kicking his feet into the lake and occasionally sending me these sullen, intense glances.

I tried again to bring him around.

"C'mon," I said, "It's too hot to argue"

"Who said anything about arguing?" said Storm, in typical fashion,

"There you go again," I said.

Storm fixed me with his sorrowful amber eyes and then said.

"You'd have a great time in Chicago"

"No, I wouldn't. You'd have a great time in Chicago. And I think you should go. But I need to stay here...."

"Need... you mean your father made you"

"No. I decided Storm. Anyway" and here I took a deep swig of the warm soda before continuing "It might be better if you and I get to spend some time apart for a bit"

That was it, that was all it took for him to look at me with those big, hurt, eyes.

"You mean you want to get away from me. Because you're scared of.... This...."

His kiss filled my lips.

But only briefly. Only for the merest second.

He must have sensed my feelings were not reciprocated.

Maybe, just for a second. But my hesitancy put out a clear enough signal to him that I was not interested.

Gently, I brushed him away.

"it's not that I'm scared Storm," I said, trying to sound as kind as possible.

And it was whilst we were there together, at that lake, on that sadistically hot summer's day that it finally happened.

I turned around and there was Storm – six feet higher into the air and breathing flames out into the atmosphere.

After months of trying and coaxing, he had finally done it. He had achieved his first shift.

Chapter 29

River

My heart was pounding in my mouth as I read Storm's description of their kiss at the lake.

It felt strange to be reading something from so long ago, from before I was born even. Yet it felt like it could have been written yesterday.

Storm's distinctive slanted handwriting still looked exactly the same as the note he had scrawled on his desk for me this morning.

In his diary, he had described perfectly the whirlwind of emotions that had built up in him on that hot, sunny day, as he attempted to kiss my dad.

Attempted seems to be the upshot of it because from what I can glean, he pulled away quickly, much to Storm's dismay.

There was more written over the page that the wind had turned for me, but I wasn't sure I should take the plunge and read it. This felt like an intrusion.

And there was something else. I suddenly could feel a strange nausea rising in my throat and a queasy feeling start in my belly.

As I've said, dragons tend to suffer from acid reflux and a whole load of assorted other digestive symptoms. Like you can probably imagine, the whole fire breathing thing plays havoc with your esophagus and it doesn't exactly do your guts a favor, either.

But this was something else. I was feeling strange fluttering sensations down there that didn't feel like a result of our tortured fire-breathing sessions - or last night's chicken biryani.

And it wasn't just the physical stuff. I was having some strange reactions to stuff just lately.

Like yesterday, I found myself feeling homesick for Carlsbad!

Right now, I was having what could only be described as an emotional reaction to the diary entry I had just read.

In fact, I was beginning to tear up.

There was something strangely touching about it. Storm's teenage hormonal lather and my dad being, well, still my dad as far as I could see - cool, calm and detached from what felt like any emotion at all.

The more things change, the more they stay the same.

And yet inside me, there was a very big change being made.

But I did not yet know what it was. All I knew was that I felt different now and reading this diary had put me into some strange sort of emotional state.

I hesitated for a moment, as the pages ruffled further with the wind blowing them open, tantalizingly, once more.

"Go on kid. Why not. You've read the rest of it, after all"

A voice startled me.

In horror, I turned abruptly around.

Of course, there was Storm Woods, practically breathing fire in front of me, his amber-flecked eyes flashing fiercely at me.

My heart almost stopped beating altogether.

"It's not what it looks like"

My mouth tried to push the pathetic excuses out, but they became charred and mumbled.

Storm looked at me mockingly.

"Sure, it isn't. Go on. Read the rest of it. Why not huh?"

Storm

No, I wasn't pissed at River reading my journal like that. Maybe I should have been but it was water under the bridge and I figured he was going to find out about all that stuff eventually.

All the same, it wouldn't hurt to make the little shit sweat it for a bit. Going around reading other people's private documents.

But the look on the kid's face was so full of terror, I practically bust a gut just trying not to laugh at him.

"Silverton said you wouldn't mind..." he stammered.

Oh, my dear boy.

I wanted to cup his perfect face in my hands and kiss him, he looked so scared.

"Really," I said, trying to keep my voice neutral. "Maybe you should read on now anyway. If it matters that much to you..."

"He seemed quite keen for me to read it" he murmured, lowering his head over the journal again.

I bet he did. The little sneak.

I can see it in his eyes. He's begging to ask me who Silverton is and what he is to me.

The thing is, that he is nothing and nobody. Not anymore. Not since River has been here – and he knows it too.

I guess he can't be taking it too well, but a guy of Silverton's age ought to know better really. It's not as if we were anything special. Not really.

What's that they call it now "friends with benefits"?

Or something like that.

I watch as River reads on, his pensive face hunched down over the hardbacked journal from all those years ago.

I think. Who the hell cares about all that now? This is what matters, the here and the now.

But... watching River discover all this for himself is just too much tempting.

So, he is beginning to ask questions about Silverton and trying to pretend that he isn't too much bothered. Fine.

Let him.

I watch him as he reads to the end of the page.

This is too much fun to stop it now.

Then he turns to me, suddenly, pale in the face.

I wonder, for a minute, if he really is taking this too seriously.

"What is it, kid? Does that answer all your questions now?"

River just grasped his stomach strangely and looked as if he was about to burp fire all over me or something.

I was about to tell him to steady on and save it for our next 'training' session when he pushed past me.

His next words weren't quite the reaction I had been expecting to hear;

"I'm going to be sick"

Chapter 30

Ashton

My phone rings. River's number, for the first time in three weeks. I have begun to worry.

His calls usually come more urgently and more frequently. He mainly complains about Storm but, as our distance grows longer, I tolerate anything that allows me to hear his voice.

However, the message I receive sounds more urgent than his typical groans.

"Dad," he sucks in his breath, "I have...I have something to tell you."

"What is it?" I ask the question calmly, thinking surely, he's run across some metropolitan inconvenience, something through which I will console him.

In the back of my mind, a few other possibilities occur to me.

That in all this time that he has been down there, in the city, with Storm, he has revealed some of our history together.

I mean, not that there is an awful lot of it to tell, truth be told. But that might not be the way that River sees it.

Or Storm for that matter. Because I was never quite sure what went on in his head, to be honest.

So, I am all ears, expecting to hear something about me and Storm.

But it doesn't come. Instead, he goes off on a completely different tack.

"Dad, is it true that shifters can, you know, have babies?"

"Yes," I answer bluntly if a little unsure. "They can. Why?"

"Well, um," he pauses. "Can they, um, get pregnant whenever?"

"I don't know the details of that, son,"

I shake my head, wondering why the boy has waited until now to ask me. Anxiety bubbles in my stomach, however, the subtle guilt of not having gathered more information myself, for not having taught him.

"What do you mean, you don't know?"

The question, punctuated by a voice in crescendo, sends my anxiety into a panic.

"In those days," I say, trying to console him, "we didn't talk about those things. Do you think your grandfather would have told me how to get other, male dragons pregnant? He and your grandmother could barely talk about regular sex."

My son huffs from the other end of the phone.

"You go on about grandma this and grandpa that. Why didn't you do something? No one said you had to do the same things they did. You have money, damn it, and you obviously have a network."

I ask myself what network he refers to, remembering my partnership with Storm. I wish I could clarify how strained said network had become before, out of a sense of duty, I put myself, once again, into contact with the man. But, as I fear my son prepares to tell me the worst, I believe such knowledge, at least for him, would prove fatal.

I reveal as much as possible.

"The network isn't really a network – understand that. I haven't kept tabs on most of the dragons of my generation."

"Why?" River's tone takes an angrier quality.

I make a half-hearted excuse.

"I've never had time. They're scattered all over the country, and possibly all over the world. The few that lived in Carlsbad never wanted to stay here, and," I pause, digesting the feeling of defeat that has begun to settle in my abdomen. "and now, I see why."

"That's great to hear, dad, just awesome, but in the end, you can't answer my question. What a help you are." River replies sarcastically, just as I suspected he would.

Throughout this difficult conversation, I appreciate that he hasn't lost his personality to the Chicago elite.

Once again out of options to help my son myself, I move to the last resort.

"You work with another dragon, you know. Have you asked him?"

I hear nothing for a while, save River's nervous breaths.

"Okay, okay. I'll ask him."

Before I can say goodbye, my son signals his farewell with a click.

Chapter 31

River

I pace in my apartment, hoping the floors, which creak ever-so-slightly under my feet, will not disturb the neighbors.

If I remember correctly from high school biology, I'm showing all the signs of pregnancy.

My stomach has been swelling gradually for the past three months and the nausea, more powerful than normal dragon acid reflux, hasn't let up. I've gained weight around my face and arms, and my skin has taken the rosy appearance that only increased blood volume could provide.

The whole situation has me in a state of panic. And my father, as usual, is of little help.

While I've made steady cash working for Storm, I don't know how it will allow me to support a child and another year at school. Furthermore, I am not sure old dad, faithful first to his beloved town and his beloved money, would allow me to return. Less so that I would ever want to return – but a lot is going to depend on how Storm takes this.

And the only other dragon either of us know well is Storm, the man likely responsible for whatever is going on in my body. Since our first night together, we have seized every opportunity to take a private moment. Emotionally, however, we've remained close colleagues at best.

Him walking in on me that night, a couple of weeks ago, when I was reading his journal was weird.

I couldn't tell whether he was about to open up on me and we were going to have some big heart to heart or if he was going to turn around and hit me.

In the end, he didn't get the chance to do either. My guts had intervened to kill the moment, as it were.

Deep down, I knew I needed to talk to Storm but didn't know how to.

So, there I was. Ringing dad.

And what was his brilliant advice – calling Storm? The man who had most likely got me into this state.

But I suppose he was right. And anyway.

Without another support system, I had little choice.

So, later that night I finally bite the bullet and resign to calling him.

I reflect, in the back of my mind, that he is charged, in the end, with helping me. Yet, I never imagined I would necessitate help such as this.

"You know it's three in the morning, don't you?" Storm answers, his voice oddly energetic and awake.

"Yes," I blush into my apartment's dimly-lit emptiness, "but I need your help."

"Listen if it's about that diary, forget it kid. It's like I said... It's the past now. Um. You don't want to know anything else, do you?" I snapped.

"It's not that it's something else, something important, I need some help with"

"Just jack off on your own," he says wryly.

"Not that. Be serious. I have a serious question."

I refuse to buy into his teasing and command him to listen. I want him to take me more seriously, especially if what I fear is true.

"Okay, shoo."

"Can male dragons get pregnant?"

"Yes." His voice sounds empty, like the tone that accompanies the blanched expressions of individuals who have become privy to disastrous news.

"Can male dragons get pregnant at any time?"

"I don't know."

I express my exasperation, wordlessly, into the receiver. Why did no one tell him the details, given his apparent affinity for illicit sexual affairs?

"Look, look," he reacts to my grunts. "My father – who raised me alone – probably told me as much as any other person in Carlsbad. Hell, it's a wonder he told me anything at all."

"Well, did he give you any other information?" I have reached the point where I will take any answers, anything to ease my worried mind.

"No, but I've done my own looking. I'm better equipped for that than your father, you know."

"I know," I respond, irritated, half at the man's – my boyfriend's? – honesty and half at his refusal to let the subject go.

"Well, I did find that male dragons can only get pregnant by other male dragons, so I would say this narrows your search quite a lot. I'm certain you've found lots of boys here in Chi-town. We're everywhere, you see."

"Dragons?"

"No, just people with pricks."

I heave a sigh of relief, then lie,

"Yes, oh yeah."

"That's good. I'm glad you've taken the time to do some...um, sampling."

He pronounces the word carefully, which leads me to wonder if he has chosen it with the same attention he gives to every detail.

He must, I assume, hint at his desire for me to remain his, to sample other thralls while never swallowing a relationship whole.

"So, what you're telling me," I return to the conversation, "is that the question of who is less important than I thought."

So, what you're telling me, I want to say, is that you, my boss, a man probably twice my age, got me pregnant.

"Yes," he replies curtly.

"Okay, um, I can get some sleep now. Bye."

"Bye-bye."

Storm blows me a kiss over the airwaves. Unsure of the sincerity of the gesture, I nevertheless kiss back.

Chapter 32

Storm

So, it appears that old dad never gave his son "the talk," at least, not a talk designed for dragons. Carlsbad has stagnated more than I imagined.

As soon as I began to show signs of interest in sex, my father, like most single fathers, decided to give me one of the most awkward talks of my life.

However, he had specialized it for dragon shifters. We were different, he told me, down to the reproductive system. Both sexes, he told me, could become pregnant. Both sexes could bear healthy children.

It was still more common for females to bear children though; however, it was possible for males to conceive and it should not be forgotten.

When this mutation – because it must have been a mutation – occurred, no one seemed to quite know.

Current dragons considered this ability an adaptation, he informed, due to the chronically low shifter populations across the globe which, as modern views had become less accepting of their kind, would only become lower.

This discussion happened over twenty years ago, but I remember well the frustrated, downcast gaze I shot toward the floor. The one perk of homosexuality in Carlsbad was not fearing fatherhood at fifteen, and not fearing adding to our already-oversaturated population of semi-sentient beings.

He also told me that doctors for dragon pregnancies were notoriously hard to find. If one of my thralls were to leave me with child, it would mean my having to all but disappear from the face of the earth for a year and a half.

I asked him what he meant by a year and a half, for he surely meant nine months.

But no, he told me, dragon pregnancies took twice as long. The body formed two bodies, essentially, during the period, but he admitted that he knew little about the biology.

Oh yes, and it was dangerous. I mean "ordinary" female pregnancies with dragon shifter babies were pretty risky enterprises on their own.

But male pregnancies were even more fraught. Not least because they had to be delivered by Caesarian section and that, for reasons of secrecy, would usually have to take place not in a hospital, but in the doctor's surgery – if you were lucky.

There were all sorts of horror stories about DIY botched operations on kitchen tables.

The upshot of all this was he scared me half stiff about the possible consequences of having unprotected sex.

Ones that put ordinary hetero sex horrors in the shade.

Just my luck, I thought. Being gay was supposed to be the get out of jail free card for pregnancy woes. Not so, being a dragon shifter meant it was still very much on the cards and then some.

My father ended our awkward chat with a stern warning to use protection and, if anyone asked, say I had tested positive for HIV at birth.

I took the warning and, for once in my life, did as I was told

Chapter 33

Storm

And now, the forgotten warning rings clear in my mind.

I should have remembered to take more care with River. I am mentally kicking myself for not remembering it.

And I don't know how dragons – male or female – show signs of fertility. Amid leaving home, starting my career, and quickly climbing the corporate ladder, I never bothered to complete the research.

In the darkness, I pray as I had when I was little when I feared some God would damn me to eternal suffering for loving other men.

At three in the morning, however, I lay in my empty bed and stare at the bluish middle-of-the-night light that streams through the cracked drapes. It makes an even line across the room, trailing from the floor, onto my comforter, and over the faint lump of my toes.

What are the odds that River has slept with another shifter? I wonder doubtfully. What are the odds, given his timid side, to go out at all?

Even I, despite having encountered several gay dragons in Chicago, don't believe they would make liberal use of River's usual haunts.

A momentary doubt casts itself over my mind; Silverton?

Mind games might be his specialty but I wasn't sure that a creepy guy twice his age like Silverton would be River's style.

Then again, he slept with me, didn't he?

But all in all, I can't take this thought seriously.

Although I wouldn't put it past Silverton to have tried something like that, I really couldn't see someone like River falling for it.

Face facts Storm, there's only one person who can realistically be in the frame for this one and it's you.

I rub my bare feet together in the sheets, which have grown soft from many washings and discolored, from many failed stain removals.

My mind dislodges from its momentary jealous fantasy between River and Silverton. It needs to concentrate on the practical, the logical and not be wrapped up in the heat and the emotion of all this.

He needs a doctor, regardless, I tell myself.

Ashton, after all, would have my head if anything became of his precious only child, especially with the chance that that child carried his heir.

Ashton. Yes. That is going to be one interesting conversation. Still. That's for another day.

First thing's first. I need to take care of River regardless.

I reach into my bedside table and thumb through a contact diary, something handed to me at my high school graduation, so many years ago. Leather-bound, it was meant to hold the names of everyone I encountered, forever.

In hindsight, I think whoever gave it to me believed – or wanted me to believe – that my world would narrow after my teens.

How wrong, but how impractical a manner to keep track of one's acquaintances. Over the years, I have taken to keeping only static numbers and names, only identities I am sure will never change.

Ironically, many of them are dragons. Thankfully, one – Marjan Septimus – is a practicing doctor.

My phone, which holds a more fluid list of contacts, also rests next to my bed. Without turning from my supine position, I tap Marjan's hours into the search engine.

Appointments begin at eight a.m. Perfect.

The digital face across from me approaches four. Normally I would lament such little sleep, but now, I eagerly await the morning. The sooner this is resolved the better.

Assuming he also hasn't hit the hay, I text young River: Take tomorrow off. I found a doctor.

Somewhere, deep in the bottom of my thoughts is the last, desperate hope that this is all a mistake on River's part and he isn't really pregnant at all.

Chapter 34

River

By giving me the day off, I thought Storm wanted me to sleep in.

But here I am, at eight a.m., barely awake and in the doctor's office. I shiver as winter's gusts finally reach my bones. There is a window in here that is wide open, despite the fact it is ardently attempting to snow outside.

One thing I can't fault Storm for is tardiness. He has acted swiftly to do something about the situation.

Whoever runs the place keeps it hidden from view, but otherwise pristine. Housed in an old building, it retains none of the cold, clinical blueness I encountered as a child when my dad would take me to the Carlsbad Clinic for my yearly checkup.

Considering the doctor knows about shifters, I encounter less uneasiness, as well. I feel no anxious rumbles in my stomach and no fire shooting into my throat, save whatever comes from the lump that has, I believe, begun to move.

Even though this lump remains safely hidden under the wrinkled, flannel shirt I pulled from my clothes pile when my boss came banging on my door, I feel self-conscious.

One other person sits in the waiting room, and I wonder if he, too, would understand what's going on.

Storm, I conclude, does not feel nervous in the least. He raises his hand over my stomach and I swat him away, just in time for a nurse to call:

"River Marsh"

I push myself up from sitting position. Storm stands as well, but I wave my hand at his face: if I can get pregnant, as strange as the idea still seems, I can see the doctor alone.

Chapter 35

River

The doctor – or Doctor Septimus, as her name badge reads – shakes my hand after I ease onto the cold examination table. Covered in paper, it does little to do away with the classic, uncomfortable doctor's office feel.

"So, River, your, um…"

"You can call him my boyfriend,"

I look down and wave my hand to my side. I feel moodier than usual, today, from the mix of little sleep and the hormones that have flooded my body.

"Alright," Dr. Septimus pencils something on my file. "Your boyfriend says you're here for some stomach trouble."

Storm said I had stomach trouble.

"Not exactly," I take up the issue slowly. "You see, I'm a…"

"You're a shifter. That's well-documented. We usually don't have people make emergency appointments here unless they are shifters; we like to keep things like that under wraps."

"Okay," I make an inward sigh of relief. "Now that that's covered, I think it's more than stomach trouble. You see, I've been nauseous in the mornings, and my stomach won't stop growing," I pull at my shirt, "I think I've gained weight, too."

The doctor doesn't miss a beat.

"So, you're telling me you think you're pregnant?"

"Yes. Yes, that's exactly what I'm telling you."

I cannot bring the word pregnant to roll off my tongue. It sounds so foreign.

Chapter 36

River

Doctor Septimus tells me to stand and follow her to another room.

"We have to do an ultrasound to make sure. The symptoms are there, but it could still be," she begins to indicate the numbers on her hands, "constipation, a tumor, dehydration, or end-stage colon cancer. It won't hurt a bit – we just need to see what's there."

I nod and shrug, for getting electromagnetic gelatin on my clothes is the least of my worries. And her cheery suggestions of terminal cancer don't phase me either.

I am pretty sure I know what is wrong with me – and as I assumed, I am not wrong.

The scan passes in a breeze but, at the end of the appointment, it is Storm who needs medical attention.

Chapter 37

Storm

Pregnant. River is pregnant.

My face turns pale from the news, and I become lightheaded on our walk to the car. I cannot start the engine after hearing River slam his door closed, behind him.

"So," I lean on the wheel and put my face in my hands. "You're pregnant."

"That's what the doctor said," he sighs.

"And your dad didn't tell you it could happen?"

"Not really," he sounds frustrated.

"He said people didn't talk about those things in his day," he makes punctuation marks in the air, "so he saw no reason to warn me. I frankly don't think he'd done much research on the topic, knowing him."

I roll my eyes. At least the boy has some grasp of the big picture.

I try to picture Ashton's face when he gets the news. How on earth is he going to take it when he finds out? When he discovers that I am responsible for this.

It is impossible to tell. Someone like Ashton just doesn't let anyone in. He could be thinking anything and I wouldn't have a clue. I never did do.

All the same, now is the time for focusing on the practical, so I say;

"Are you going to tell him? You can't hide it forever."

"I plan to," he crosses his arms over his stomach, "but I just can't right now."

River stares out the window, and I start the car. Over the course of the morning, the cold sky has clouded over, showing rain on the horizon.

He might be the one who is pregnant, but right then, I am the one who has come over all queasy. I can barely feel my foot on the gas pedal. It is as if I am going to throw up.

I feel strangely lightheaded.

I am forced to wind the window right down and take in some air, even though it is bitterly cold outside.

Drops patter on my windowpane as I drive River, not to his apartment, but mine. His blue eyes, now flat, tell me he needs some company.

Chapter 38

Ashton

It's the middle of the day, and work calls my name.

It's been a few days since River's momentous phone call and although I haven't been able to stop thinking about it, I've done my damnedest to try.

I have had the excuse of work to keep me busy.

Yet, focus escapes me. My mind just won't stop wandering in the way of River's last call. I, the man who should have known everything, the man who should have given his child all the information necessary for success, has failed.

So, instead of working, I sit before my computer. I haven't used it for the Internet in God knows how long. Fortune will have me if it still works.

But the search engine speeds into life. In its single, white-framed box, I type:

Dragon male pregnant

I find I have underestimated the number of results such terms would draw forth. I go narrower:

Dragon male pregnant by another male dragon

I scroll through several shock headlines involving lizards before I come upon my desired results. I click on the first page that seems credible, and then on another.

Everything confirms what I have feared.

After mine and River's worried exchange: male dragons can become pregnant by other male dragons and, unlike with female dragons, the time of ovulation happens at less regular intervals.

Why the hell has it taken me so long to check out this vital fact.

Well, I guess I was scared. Scared and in denial.

I put my head in my hands. River was right, and he had every right to be angry.

The answers to his questions were only an internet search away, and I ignored them. And by ignoring them, I ignored him.

I pull my phone out of my pocket and dial his number. I have an apology to make.

River

It's been a strange few days.

Storm hasn't been going into the office recently and seems to have taken up residence beside me. Part of me wonders how long this newfound attentiveness will last.

Right now, he lies snuggled at my side, asleep after a cup of coffee that turned into an hour-long lovemaking session. I, myself marvel at how I am still awake.

My father's number flickers on my phone screen, an odd thing to find in the middle of what, for him, would be a work day. He's the last person I want to talk to but, nonetheless, I pick up.

"I'm sorry, son. I thought you would have thought,"

His voice echoes through the phone, and I cannot believe what I hear. I sit up in the bed, allowing Storm's head to slide off my shoulder.

"Well, I didn't know," I tell him, with more force and authority. "I thought you would tell me."

I notice I've become more assertive since arriving in Chicago. I attribute this change to the busy city atmosphere, as well as the clogged traffic that, initially, didn't pose a problem.

But now, rush hour traffic is the least of my worries. And the pangs of homesickness that I have been feeling, have grown larger with my belly over the recent weeks.

I'm pregnant.

Storm's ministrations can only distract me for a minute, but I still cannot imagine having a small child of my own. Probably a shifter itself, it will be running around my apartment – or wherever I live – in eighteen months.

I'm single, as far as everyone at the interior design firm is concerned, and I'm barely on the edge of twenty-two. I scarcely know how to cook. How could I take care of a kid?

How the hell am I going to hide it, for a start off?

Not everyone there is a shifter, after all.

Come to think about it, it is the shifters from whom I have got to be the most careful... even in this day and age, no one is really going to think that a man could be pregnant.

But to other shifters – ones who have been told all the facts of life by their parents, that is – they might be on the lookout for the signs.

Someone like Silverton will definitely notice.

Silverton.

There is someone who seems to be disappearing from view, at least as far as Storm is concerned.

Since I have dropped the bombshell, he seems to have been playing a lesser role in the business – and around Storm.

I think the current excuse is that he is away on business – an ideal home exhibition in Paris. But I can't pretend that his absence has not been welcomed by me.

I'm actually not too fussed what the old weasel and Storm get up to. Really, I'm not. I just can do without his greasy presence and the faint whiff of patchouli that follows him about everywhere.

Apart from anything else, it is making me nauseous.

Smells, in particular, have really become troublesome since becoming pregnant. I had no idea that pregnancy was like this.

Stroking my belly, I wonder idly if all pregnancies are like this or just shifter ones. But there is no one I can ask.

It would be nice if I could talk to my dad. At least find out what he can remember about my mom's experiences with me. But he's not here and a phone call isn't the same thing as being there, face to face.

Heaven knows, he doesn't open up to me much about anything, far less her.

It occurs to me as I sit there, musing on my expanding midriff, that she must have been the thing to come between him and Storm.

And although from scanning Storm's account of it – which I did do, right beneath his curious amber gaze – he blamed the cessation of their relationship on my grandfather. Reading between the lines, it is clear to see this was not the case at all.

As far as I could tell from what he wrote about my father, Storm never had that sort of a relationship with him and my dad simply chose my mother over him.

It must have hurt, especially for someone with an ego the size of a planet.

How I would have liked to be able to talk to him about this right now, but over the telephone, it just isn't possible to get the words out.

The independence offered by this Chicago trip no longer feels so liberating. I want to move closer to home, closer to the man who, despite his mistakes, has known me best.

"I didn't tell you, and it was wrong. I didn't honor your curiosity, and I didn't respect your sexuality,"

The apology comes slow and hesitant. Of course, it also comes punctuated with;

"Do you know who it's with?" as though I've hooked up with a whole network of gay dragon shifters in the Chicago area.

"Dad," I tell him, "I think it's pretty obvious who I'm having this kid with."

A pause.

A silence that deepens and grows.

I wait fearfully, as the implications of what I have just said sink in.

But in the end, instead of fireworks, there is merely a sigh.

My dad groans;

"He strikes again, the bastard. Storm has a – how should I put it – he tends to get around. I should have warned you."

Perhaps he's not happy. That would be too much to hope for. He sounds resigned if anything.

But accepting.

Just about.

I think.

"No warning needed," I promise. "Everything was consensual,"

I tell only optimistic half-truths to ease dad's mind. I don't tell him we're official, and I avoid recounting our occasional spats. I have to keep our relationship professional, to retain some respect in my family's – or perhaps, Carlsbad's – eyes.

"So, you've told him?" My father asks anxiously. "He's okay with it?"

"Yes," I say quietly, so as not to wake my sleeping lover.

"I've told him. I have to go, now, it's a busy day," I lie, "I'll see you sometime."

"Yeah, if I can get a vacation," he half-jokes. "But really, I'd love to see the little tyke."

"Oh yeah," I cringe inwardly at the thought of giving birth, even if that day is several months away. "Definitely. I love you."

"Love you, too."

Chapter 39

Ashton

Storm's eyes flutter open as soon as I hang up the phone.

"Everything resolved?"

"Yes, or kind of. He figured out for himself how male dragons get pregnant, one way or another."

Storm rolls his eyes and turns onto his stomach;

"Yeah, technology is a marvelous thing."

My hand strays into his hair, a long, silky black mass that, shaken loose, frames his pale face. He moves closer to me and, seizing the opportunity, kisses my swollen stomach.

"You're going to make a cute pregnant person, you know," he raises an eyebrow. "I'm going to have to put you away, keep the other guys from taking you."

"Oh right, like anyone would want to fuck a pregnant man. How would I even explain it?"

Storm shrugs. "Sometimes, there's no explanation necessary."

In the ridiculousness of it all, I laugh.

Chapter 40

River

The following weekend, Storm has me in the woods, again. His original personality has made a comeback, as well as his sleek, professional, and comparatively cold persona.

"I need you to put more fire in it," he shouts across the field. "Give it more push."

Fire-breathing remains the priority, the thing to perfect. My acid reflux makes the task less difficult but, according to my trainer, it needs more elegance.

"A professional dragon doesn't spit fire everywhere. They stick to a target. What's your target?"

I stare at another branch, full of dying, fall leaves. This, I decide, will have to be my target until I find something worth targeting. Storm told me that some dragons focus on small animals, like rats, when learning how to breathe fire. For me, the boy who never went hunting, this idea approaches inhumane.

"A deep inhale, now."

I follow his instructions, as though I haven't a million times before.

"And another exhale."

As has been the case, fire comes out, this time. While nothing, from what I observe, differs greatly from this time and my first tentative attempt, I register an approving nod from my partner. After the flames die down, he calls,

"That's enough for today. You can shift back, now."

Chapter 41

River

Although I mark Storm's return to his rather-stagnant self, our lovemaking has taken an entirely different tone since news of my pregnancy. Instead of our usual one-timers, Storm and I both muster the stamina to endure the three – even four – rounds necessary to satisfy our needs.

I imagine this must do, in part, with the fact that we have taken to living together – at least part of the time - and know each other better.

My dragon intuition, too, factors into the equation. It has improved since my confused and awkward arrival.

Storm's abrupt end to our training, as well as the speed with which he scampers out of sight while I shift back, tells me he needs something other than simple affection. After cleaning the campsite, I follow Storm into his driver's side door and straddle my legs across his lap.

"God," he moans. "How did you know?"

"Well," I whisper, "It isn't every day we get to be this alone."

I place soft kisses upon his neck and moan myself. He loves displays of want.

Chapter 42

River

I kiss and bite for a time that feels like several minutes, waiting for him to have his way with me.

However, that time never comes.

"I need you," Storm moans instead. "I need you to master me."

I jump slightly, surprised by the command.

Storm senses my shock. He sends his piercing orange gaze into mine.

"You heard what I said."

Chapter 43

Storm

If I knew he planned to act on his feelings, I would have told him to not bother dressing.

The slide of his legs across my lap sends tingles down my spine, as well as an involuntary gasp that pushes from my lower abdomen.

So, I think, he's finally learned. After several months, he has reached a level of confidence that allows him to straddle me, to tell me, with his body, he wants me.

And I want him. No – I should stay submissive – I need him. I need him to stay on top of me, I need him to conquer my lust.

I tell him exactly that.

He unbuttons my shirt obediently, offering gentle kisses as he exposes my bare torso to the sun-warmed interior of the van. His stomach is pressed against my own and I instinctively hold it, pressing my hands lightly over the child that belongs to me – to us.

He reaches his hand over my member, then retracts. I hear his pants unzip and, before me, he wields his own erection. He runs his hand over it, sending glistening pre-cum over the tip.

I want that inside me, damn it, but, in a true commanding fashion, the boy merely teases in response to my request. He pleasures himself, rocking onto his knees and supporting his back against the steering wheel. Desperate, I lean forward and try to take him, any part of him, into my mouth.

The boy soon glides his length onto my begging tongue.

"If only you could see yourself", he chides, "my boss, touching himself and sucking his little assistant's cock."

I whimper, but this is the language I've searched for. I undo my own pants, for rubbing can only satisfy so much exterior stimulation.

At the same time, he pushes my head over his member.

"Deeper," he groans, "deeper..."

A little time passes before we both enter the throes of passion. In a satisfied wave of pleasure, I thank the skies that I, finally, have been mastered.

Chapter 44

River

Over the past three months, Storm, with the help of some of his more sensitive coworkers has put together an adequate nursery.

It has been difficult, knowing exactly who we can be honest with and who must be kept in the dark. Since my belly has grown ever larger, I have been under practical house arrest, back here at my apartment.

Storm keeps trying to coax me into his place – I'm spending more time there - but just for now, it doesn't feel right.

I don't want to impose upon him.

The fact he has taken it this well has astonished me, but I am assuming he is acting mainly out of a sense of duty than anything else.

"But the colors," he argues with me over Sunday brunch, "just don't go."

"It's for a baby," I tell him, laughing. "It's not supposed to go. A nursery makes the kid comfortable. It doesn't show them the latest design trends." I roll my eyes, "We can always paint it when the kid gets older."

"Yes, older, and already ruined by bad taste." He spreads the last of the butter on a piece of toast, which he cuts into small slices.

I pour myself another cup of coffee.

Thank goodness, I think, that the parental instincts have kicked in for one of us.

Chapter 45

River

Dad calls later that afternoon. We have talked some over text, but haven't communicated since he found out about the pregnancy.

"I just got word from your school. Apparently, you haven't registered for next semester?"

"That's kind of impossible, dad," I correct. "I don't know how I would fit a baby in a dorm room."

I'm not surprised of my need to remind him that, yes, I'm expecting. It isn't anything someone from Carlsbad – or, perhaps, anyone from Chicago – would believe.

Dad sighs on the other end of the phone.

"You're right. What should I tell them?"

"That I'm taking the semester off," I clarify.

I'm thinking how strange some small-town customs have become. In cases such as mine, no one needs a detailed explanation. No one needs to know your whole life.

"Is that it?"

"Yes, that's it."

In his typical, workaholic fashion, he hangs up without saying goodbye.

Chapter 46

River

My stomach has grown considerably, even after only a month. In the evening, I sit in the living room, in semi-darkness, running my hands over its domelike form.

"Does it feel strange?" Storm asks, shuffling into the room and turning on a table lamp.

At home he seems calmer, returning to his normal state after having performed for his peers.

"Not exactly. Just different. I feel like there's something attached to me."

When I was little, old women, usually the ones at church, told me that pregnancy happened after eating a watermelon seed. They told me that the seed grew inside a woman's stomach, and then transformed into a baby.

But I haven't felt full of watermelon, or anything else. For the most part, I feel like I've created another compartment within me, all the while becoming more ravenous.

Storm pulls me out of my thoughts.

"Do you feel attached to the baby?"

"Yes, physically and emotionally."

The man rubs his eyes.

"This is going to sound weird and shamefully mushy, but I feel the same."

"Really?"

I assumed that he felt some sort of duty in taking me in, both as a boyfriend and as my father's old friend. I wouldn't have predicted him to be so fond of his seed.

Although my heart kind of leaps when he says this, I try and hold myself back a little.

We have never really spoken like this before. Despite everything.

Our conversations have been practical only in nature, about where I will live and how the baby will be delivered.

Naturally, I am doing a lot of skulking around at home, under the pretext of having glandular fever – or is it scarlet?

I can't quite remember what the excuse was, that Storm presented to the office to explain my absence.

All I do know is that I have found myself with a lot of time on my hands, suddenly, to think about things and I have discovered two things;

I love this baby already and... I think that I might love Storm as well.

But the second part of this is something that I have completely given up on.

Storm is a free spirit. I have recognized that now.

Just because he seems to have suddenly quit going out clubbing and spending all hours out with other men, doesn't mean I am expecting anything.

It's ok; I am resigned to it.

So, what he says next both surprises and shocks me completely.

"Yes, and I guess you could say I'm attached to you, as well."

His eyes, from across the room, seem warm. Full, even, when touched with the lamp's warm colors.

This is not something that I have been expecting to hear. In fact, I can't actually believe that I have heard it right the first time.

"Pardon," I say primly, making Storm laugh out loud.

But he clears his throat and tries again, taking my hand softly.

"I'll be with you through this, you know."

I nod, then stare into the living space. My heart is racing fast now.

So much has changed, in less than a year.

Looking at the man across from me, however, I see it has changed for the better: Storm encapsulates someone who has overcome the fears Carlsbad created, from homosexuality to his own dragon identity.

Storm takes my hand more forcefully now;

"I won't let you down, you can guarantee it River."

"I know," I say quietly, the emotion rising in my voice, as I try to dampen it down.

I pray I can become half the man he is, and that I can teach our child to be the same.

*****

Don't miss out!

Visit the website below and you can sign up to receive emails whenever Van Cole publishes a new book. There's no charge and no obligation.

https://books2read.com/r/B-A-RTRV-MZXCC

BOOKS 2 READ

Connecting independent readers to independent writers.

Also by Van Cole

3 Man Huddle: MMM Best Friend Romance
His Alpha Wolf: Gay First Time Romance
A Dragon's Miracle: Gay Dragon MPREG Romance
Double-Teamed: MMM First Time Football Romance
His Football Star: Gay Second Chance Romance
Love In My Town: MM First Time Romance
Training A Hockey Star
Game Night
Double Shift
Take A Shot
Dear Professor
Getting Inked
Ninth Inning
Triple Threat
Seducing My Best Friend's Brother
My Protector
The Blueprint
Show Me The Way
End Zone
Matched To His Tiger
Love At First Puck
My Straight Boss
Falling For The Alpha
My Boss
On Thin Ice

www.ingramcontent.com/pod-product-compliance
Lightning Source LLC
Chambersburg PA
CBHW021206160726
47994CB00001B/364